SWITCHED

a novel

Angela Lam

Gross Productions

For anyone who has felt like a foreigner in their own body.

United States, the near future

CHAPTER 1

Maxine slung her backpack over her shoulders and tiptoed down the staircase and across the kitchen floor. Early morning sunlight streamed through the dining room window. In the adjacent living room, her mother sat on a sofa, listening to the morning-show hosts mutter warnings about the end of the world, for everyone was changing—man to woman, old to young—and no one could do anything to stop it.

"Armageddon," one of the hosts said.

Holding her breath, Maxine stiffened. Her best friend, Patty, had recently changed from a young college student to an elderly man.

"Where you going so early?"

Maxine yelped, releasing her breath, her heart rate racing in her chest.

Her mother loomed in the doorway like an apparition glowering between this world and the next.

"You scared me," Maxine said, placing a hand on her chest.

"Serves you right for leaving without saying a word."

Maxine didn't want to argue with her mother. It was all they had done since *the change* had started. Older feminists squawked about the appropriation of the perimenopausal phrase to describe the ungodly phenomenon afflicting certain segments of the population. But until a scientific name was given, the colloquial one, appropriated or not, would do.

"Well?" Her mother tapped her foot. "I'm waiting."

The morning-show hosts' voices carried into the room, buffering the silence.

An insidious tension coiled throughout Maxine's body. The way her mother's eyebrows pinched together made her feel like an errant child and not a twenty-two-year-old college senior. She tucked her chin toward her chest. She was a small woman, barely five feet, but her mother's anger and disapproval made her feel even smaller. If she were a great actress, she could make up a story, and her mother would believe her. But Maxine's body quivered like a plucked string whenever she fibbed, so she resigned herself to the truth.

"I'm picking up Patty and taking her to breakfast before our first class."

"You seem to be spending a lot of time with old people. Men especially."

Not this again. Maxine's hands curled into fists. "Mom, Patty's a woman, trapped in a man's body."

"Yeah, I know. That's why you shouldn't be spending time with her." Her mother spread her arms wide and lifted her shoulders like she was a prophet calling upon God. "Who knows if she's contagious?"

From what Maxine had read, the change wasn't a virus or something that could be transmitted from person to person. Scientists couldn't pinpoint or explain why the phenomenon only happened to certain people under certain circumstances at certain times. To her, it all seemed random. To her mother, it seemed like a medical version of manifest destiny.

"I won't catch it, I promise." Maxine crossed her fingers behind her back in the event the change happened to her someday.

A low grumble erupted from her mother's stomach.

An idea blossomed, and Maxine smiled. "I'll make you coffee and toast before I leave."

Food was always a bribe. She hoped it worked.

Her mother beamed. "That's my girl." She patted her shoulder before shuffling to the living room.

In the kitchen, Maxine set her backpack on the tiled counter and unzipped a pocket, searching for her cell phone.

Years ago, people had had to type their messages into their phones until a company—one her boyfriend, Joe, had founded—developed the technology to translate one's thoughts into texts. Now he was working on brain-to-brain software so you could think directly with others—no device or implant needed. Maxine wished the technology were already available so she wouldn't have to deal with her phone. But the Federal Communications Commission had not approved its release.

Sighing, Maxine sent a thought-to-text to Patty to let her know she had been delayed, but would be there as soon as possible. Maybe fifteen minutes later than promised. Next, Maxine filled the carafe with water and poured it into the coffee maker. She scooped two heaping tablespoons of ground beans into the filter and flicked the machine on. Within seconds, the coffee maker burbled and burped. She untwisted the tie from a loaf of sourdough bread—the soft kind that the grocery stores sold—and placed two pieces into the toaster.

Her phone pinged with a reply. Maxine read the text as she waited for the coffee to percolate and the toast to warm and brown. Patty would be waiting outside on the porch. Indignation burned in the pit of Maxine's stomach. She always believed Patty's parents were more reasonable than hers were. At least more reasonable than her mother. Her father—when he had been alive—always championed her causes and wouldn't have allowed her to be treated like a leper if she had changed from a young woman into an old man. Obviously, Patty's parents were more like her mother—full of fear and pity.

The coffee maker sputtered until the dark liquid stopped dribbling, and the golden-brown pieces of bread popped out of the toaster.

Maxine poured a mug full of rich-smelling coffee and drizzled maple syrup over two pieces of toast and sprinkled them with cinnamon and powdered sugar. After grabbing a fork, a knife, and a cloth napkin from a drawer, she placed everything on a tray and carried it into the living room, where her mother slouched on the sofa, her gaze riveted on the images on the TV. Some medical experts were talking about the change, which was now being referred to as "the switch" since it caused people to flip-flop ages and genders. This expert suggested it might be the result of some alien invasion that had scrambled our DNA while we slept.

"Oh, thank you, child," her mother said, inhaling deeply. She snatched the napkin and laid it over her lap before cutting a slice of the cinnamon toast and tucking it into her mouth. "Mmm-mmm. You sure cook good, girl. Your daddy would be proud. God rest his soul."

Hmph. Her dead father would have been proud, but her living mother wasn't. Why was it always easier to please the dead than the living? Tension knotted in her gut.

"Bye, Mom." Maxine bent to kiss the top of her mother's head. The hair tasted greasy and smelled like wilted flowers. "I'll see you after my last class ends."

"I've joined The Revolution," Patty said.

Maxine glanced up from cutting her chicken fried steak and met her friend's steady gaze. The face she stared at had changed from the soft skin and chubby cheeks of young adulthood to the leathery skin and wrinkles of old age. But the eyes, steel gray and strong, retained the same indefatigable determination to right all the wrongs in the world. She didn't know what to say. In a way, she had joined her own revolution, FIRE—financial independence, retire early. That was why she lived with her mother (to save money) and why she dated Joe (to learn the skills not taught in school so she could make enough money by thirty to never work again).

"I want you to join too," Patty said.

"I don't want to die." Maxine slipped the wedge of meat into her mouth and chewed, her hands still holding the fork and knife—weapons in her war against her best friend.

She had seen the protesters on TV, picketing and rioting. Clouds of tear gas and armed police officers arresting old men who had once been young women. Across the nation, people were dying—if not from old age, then from The Revolution.

Patty lifted one shoulder in a shrug and grabbed the mug of steaming coffee. She wore her father's shirt, but her chest and shoulders weren't broad enough to fill the space, and the leftover material sagged around her old-man body. "We all die one way or another. Why not fight for what is right?"

She puckered her lips to take a sip, but with the lack of coordination in her aging fingers, she missed the opening, and a few drops dribbled down her shirt. Cussing, she clattered the mug against the table, seized the cloth napkin, dipped it into the glass of iced water, and dabbed the spot, trying to prevent a stain.

All around them, the early morning patrons ate in the twenty-four-hour diner they had frequented since high school. The food was mediocre, and the ambiance lacked originality, but the servers were quick, and the prices were affordable. Maxine loved the smells of bacon and eggs and maple syrup that hung in the air like a constant haze and the booths with the comfortable, upholstered cushions and big windows overlooking the parking lot.

Over the years, she and Patty had come here to share secrets and confessions, hopes and dreams, fears and failures. When Maxine's father died while she was in high school, she came here with Patty. Maxine cried over a thick vanilla milkshake, topped with whipped cream and cookie crumbles, while Patty rubbed her back and told her everything would be all right. When Patty switched, she came here with Maxine. Between bites of a burger, Patty had railed against the conspiracy to eliminate the human race while Maxine stole a handful of fries from her plate.

"What do you hope to accomplish?" Maxine asked.

"Force the universities to fund research to find a cure."

"You can't force anyone to do anything."

Patty tossed the napkin on the table. "With enough pressure, the universities will cave. University of California Los Angeles gave in last week. Why not Sonoma State University?"

Maxine had read enough and witnessed enough to

know that no one knew why anyone was switching, so how could anyone find a cure? "So, what if SSU eventually concedes and donates all its resources toward research? How long will it take to pinpoint the cause of the switch?"

"I don't know. But it can't be that long. We've found cures for other things in a handful of months. I could be back to myself by Christmas."

"But you'll miss bikini season." Maxine winked, hoping to lighten the mood.

"Ha-ha, very funny," Patty sneered.

A server asked if they wanted more coffee. Patty nodded, and Maxine shook her head.

Just the two of them again, Patty stirred more creamer into her mug. "I don't care who's responsible. Something must be done to fix this problem." She stopped moving her spoon, but the coffee kept swirling. Her whole body quivered, and her eyes filled with tears. "I want my body back."

The trembling voice cut through Maxine's resistance, and she stretched an arm across the table and squeezed her friend's hand. "I know you do. I do too. I miss our sleepovers." Her mother had stopped letting Maxine spend the night after Patty switched. "But what if no one can give you that body back? Then what will you do?"

Patty blinked, and her eyes cleared. "I don't know, but whatever it is, I'll die trying."

CHAPTER 2

Maxine sat in the cool, dark college auditorium, listening to the art history professor drone on and on about ancient artifacts during the Roman Empire while showing slides of broken pots projected against the wall. Most of her classmates huddled in their stadium chairs with sweatshirts draped across their shoulders. A few students typed notes for next month's final exam on their laptops. A couple of students dozed, their snores punctuating the lecture like the chorus of a song. Maxine pretended to pay attention while her thoughts drifted. She was a business major, and her only interest in art was its commercial value.

From her backpack, her phone pinged. She lurched in her chair, scrambling with the zipper. How could she have forgotten to mute the ringer? With her finger, she swiped the screen. Joe had sent a thought-to-text, saying she was on his mind. Super sweet of him. She sent him a kissy-face emoji before she turned the ringer to vibrate and tossed the phone into her open backpack.

The professor moved on to a new slide and discussed the details of a different piece of pottery. Maybe if he had an appealing voice—varied, not monotone—Maxine might have focused. But his voice only provided white noise for her imagination. She envisioned the underpaid, overworked archaeologists at the dig with their construction equipment, blasting away the big pieces of rock and chiseling away the finer pieces of stone until uncovering the artifact. Archaeologists, in her opinion, weren't any better than gravediggers. They both profited from the past.

She shifted in her seat and stifled a yawn. No wonder she had delayed taking this general education course until her last semester. There was no point in studying history. It did not, from what she could see, repeat itself. She believed, as a species, they would be better off if they could leave the past alone, buried and forgotten, something best ignored. What mattered was the future. Take that army of archaeologists and retrain them to identify and prevent something like the switch from happening, and humanity would be better served.

Her phone vibrated in her backpack. She was jolted to attention. After grabbing the phone and swiping the screen, she felt a spike of hope. Not a text, but an email from the university's recruiting department. An interview had been arranged for her with a telecommunications company next week. As soon as she recognized the name of Joe's rival, her jaw stiffened. The CEO needed a right-hand person, and the recruiter hoped it would be Maxine.

She dropped the phone in her lap and wiped the sweat from her palm. Her pulse pounded in her throat, and her mouth went dry. She fumbled with the phone, trying to compose a thought-to-text in the dark auditorium while the professor mumbled on and on about a fractured vase, presented on yet another slide. As the words formed in her mind, they appeared as text on her phone.

—*Sorry to decline. Conflict of interest. Please keep me in mind for similar positions in other industries.—*

Class ended.

The lights flicked on, and Maxine blinked until her vision adjusted to the shock. Her hand still gripped the phone. She gathered her belongings and exited Stevenson Hall. The explosion of natural sunlight caught her off guard, and she stumbled for a few steps until her sight adapted and she regained her balance.

She sent a thought-to-text to Joe.

—Had an offer for an interview with your rival. Declined. Could you reconsider asking the board for a policy exception to hire me? Need a job ASAP. Tired of living at home.—

Ahead, a group of students had gathered with signs, picketing the switch.

Most people ignored them, skirting around the group that milled on the lawn and spilled on the sidewalks, dodging their chants that rose and evaporated like mist.

Maxine squinted, searching for Patty. She glimpsed her in the center of the crowd, marching, her old-man arm holding a sign high in the air—*Give me back my body*—as if the command alone could evoke a reverse transformation, like putting a genie back into a bottle.

A cool breeze picked up, and Maxine shuddered. She found a spot on a bench, away from the protesters, and plunked her backpack on the wooden slats. After finding her sweatshirt, she tugged it over her head and adjusted the sleeves. She had an hour until her next class started on the other side of campus. She hoisted the backpack over her shoulders and strode away from the picketing students, the sounds of their cries like popcorn tossed against her back. But she didn't turn. She refused to acknowledge them. For what good would it do?

None. Whatever was happening was outside of anyone's control, and the only thing to do was ignore it.

CHAPTER 3

The sun had skipped across the sky by the time Maxine exited her last class. Four hours since she had sent her text, and she had not heard back from Joe. Worry pinched her chest. He usually responded promptly, between meetings, or during lunch. As she strode across the campus, she called his office and spoke with Heather, his executive assistant, who told her he had not called in sick or come into the office today.

Now her concern ratcheted up a notch. She picked up her pace, hoping to drive by his house on the way home. She didn't have a key, but she could knock on the front door. But would he answer? Of course he would. Wouldn't he? Unless he was too sick. Too sick to respond with a text. Too sick to walk to the door.

She halted in the center of campus. Oh my. The protesters still littered the lawn, their chants rising like steam. The numbers had grown from this morning, doubling or maybe even tripling, their signs raised high like flags.

"Stop the switch! Give us back our bodies!"

Maxine heard the anguish in their voices. She felt bad for them, but she knew their efforts were pointless. The university couldn't help them. No one could.

She studied the mass of bodies, searching for a safe

passage to the other side.

"Maxine!" Patty waved, holding up a sign.

Instinctively, Maxine rushed toward her, hoping her friend might find a way to thread her through the marching picketers so she could get to her car in the adjacent parking lot. But before she could reach Patty's side, her friend collapsed, and the mob swallowed her.

Maxine yelped. She jostled forward, nudging protesters with her elbows, her backpack swinging from her shoulders, but the wall of humanity erected before her would not budge.

In the distance, sirens blared.

What was happening to the world? All around her, people pushed and shoved—a stampede of wild animals, full of fear and panic. Maxine struggled to catch a glimpse of her downed friend through the crowd, but no matter how much she ducked and dodged, she could not move forward or backward or sideways. A geyser of tears erupted, and she swatted at her leaky face, vision blurred, still pressing against the tide of people, but there was no way she could reach Patty, no way at all.

Two hours and several arrests later, the crowd had thinned and dispersed, leaving nothing but a mess of abandoned signs and litter that Maxine stepped around as she made her way to the parking lot on the other side of campus.

She didn't know where the paramedics had taken Patty. She tried calling the landline at Patty's parents' house, but a constant busy signal blared in her ear. She wished she had their cell numbers, but who asked for the cell phone numbers of their friends' parents?

The sun had inched its way toward the horizon, and remnants of light striped the pavement. After the terror and chaos of the chanting protesters and shouting megaphones from the police, the silence rang like a hollow bell.

Safe in the confines of her car, she sent Joe a thought-to-text, telling him what little she knew about what had happened to Patty. When he didn't respond, she drove to his neighborhood, an established subdivision with wide streets and mature cypress trees. The picturesque beauty contrasted heavily with the violence and confusion of the campus riots. She parked on the street, squinting at the curtained windows, and wondered if Joe was inside, sick and asleep. She didn't want to wake him, but after what she had just witnessed, she needed to know he was okay.

When no one responded to her constant ringing and knocking, she skirted around the house, searching for an open window or an unlocked back door, but everything was closed. As the streetlights flicked on, she tugged the gate to the backyard closed and strode to her car. She glanced at the time. Eight thirty. She could wait, or she could go home.

From her backpack, Maxine removed a protein bar and a thermos of water. She ate the makeshift dinner in the front seat of her car, her gaze trained between the street and the front yard.

At nine fifteen, a car pulled into the driveway, and a young woman stepped out of the vehicle. She circled around to the trunk, removed several shopping bags, and waved goodbye to the driver who pulled out into the street.

Who is she? Maxine squinted, trying to determine whether she knew the blonde who struggled up the porch steps in kitten heels.

When the woman unlocked the front door and disappeared inside, Maxine gasped. No wonder Joe hadn't returned her calls and text messages. He had ghosted her for this freakishly tall model who couldn't walk a straight line in heels.

A flurry of questions erupted in her mind. *How long has Joe been dating this woman? Has she moved in with him?* Maxine gulped a mouthful of air, and her heartbeat crashed against her ribs. *Are they married?*

All her mother's worst fears pelted her. *Don't date a man old enough to be your father. Don't trust a divorced man. Don't believe anything rich people say.*

Don't, don't, don't.

But she did, did, did.

And now a thick, hot sweat doused her in regret. She tore off the sweatshirt and mopped her forehead. Her phone pinged.

She sniffed, trying hard not to cry. No man was worth crying over. That was what her mother said. Maxine had always thought her mother would have been better off if she had cried after her husband died, but what did Maxine know? She was young and stupid. Falling for a man old enough to be her father. Father! She rubbed the edge of her sweatshirt's sleeve against the corner of her eyelid before she rummaged in her backpack for her phone.

A quick swipe revealed a message from Joe, who had probably been woken by the live-in woman—she couldn't think of her as a wife or girlfriend, not yet—who didn't care that he had lain in bed sick all day, perhaps near dying, too weak to pick up his phone to call anyone, not even the office.

—*Sorry to respond so late. Left phone at home by accident.*—

Yeah, sure, she scoffed. *You've been home all day.*

Her phone pinged with a response. She widened her eyes. She hadn't meant to send a thought-to-text. Damn phone. She swiped the screen and read his reply.

—*I left at ten and just came home a few moments ago.*—

She tried to modulate her breathing, unwilling to send a thought-to-text, but the words flew across her mind.

—*That's a lie.*—

—*I'm not lying.*—

—*Then who is the woman who just entered your house?*—

Silence.

She glowered at the dark windows of his home. The bedroom faced the backyard. She wondered if the young woman had turned on the lights. Maybe she could sneak a peek through the plantation shutters. She palmed her phone, her thoughts stewing in the worst-case scenario —the young woman, naked in bed with Joe, who wasn't sick, but taking a day off for what, she didn't know, and their bodies tangled in a heated mess of arms and legs and God knew what else, maybe some kinky stuff she wouldn't ever want to try. Was that why he had dumped her? She heaved a sigh. What if she was right? The situation would remain unchanged. She was still a ghosted woman, a betrayed woman, a woman unknowingly caught in a love triangle. She tossed her phone on the seat and started the engine.

Her phone rang.

She pulled away from the curb and drove. The call

continued to ring through the stereo speakers. Her hands shook too much to grab her phone off the seat, so she jabbed the button on her steering wheel without knowing who it was—Patty, her mom, Joe, or the other woman.

"Hello?"

"Don't hang up. It's Joe."

The high-pitched voice sounded squeaky. Was this the other woman calling to harass her? She lowered her foot against the brakes, slowing for a speed bump. Her heartbeat ratcheted in her chest. What did you say to your lover's secret wife or girlfriend? If she had just listened to her mother, she would have avoided this mess. Maybe if she apologized, the young woman would leave her alone, and she could go on with her life. Yeah, it would be tough, and she'd miss him, but it wasn't the end of the world. There were plenty of available men her own age.

"I'm sorry—"

"Why are *you* sorry? *I'm* sorry for not being there when you needed me today. Is Patty okay?"

Her jaw stiffened. How long had this other woman been reading Joe's messages? "I don't know why you're doing this to me." Her voice hitched.

"Because I care."

"You care?" She laughed, braking at the stoplight. "Why do you care that Joe hurt me?"

"I *am* Joe." The exasperation in the woman's voice echoed throughout the car. "I've switched."

Switched?

The light turned green, and Maxine waited a second too long before releasing the brakes, and the light turned yellow, then red again.

"That's why I wasn't here or at work or anywhere I

would normally be. I had to get some clothes and some tampons. I didn't want to bother you, not after what you went through with Patty, so I called my ex-wife. We spent all day shopping." He groaned. "I'm exhausted. I don't know how you women do it. On your feet all day, rifling through sales racks, searching for things that go together, and trying everything on. Not to mention the makeup, and the skin care, and the mani-pedi, and the eyebrow waxing. Ugh. My face still hurts." He paused to take a breath. "I'm sorry, baby. I should have called when it happened this morning. I tried. I sent a thought-to-text, letting you know I was thinking of you. But I chickened out. I figured you might dump me now that I'm a woman. And I can't live without you." His voice wavered. "I'm so, so sorry."

She listened, and her hands slackened around the steering wheel. When the light turned green, she made an illegal U-turn and headed back down his street. The strange car. The shopping bags. The inability to walk in heels. Everything made sense now.

"Maxine?"

"I'm coming over." She ended the call.

The car rumbled over speed bumps. She was driving too fast, eager to confirm her suspicions.

After parking in the same spot she had recently vacated, she grabbed her backpack, locked her car, marched up the walkway to the porch, and rang the doorbell.

The front door unlocked, and the young woman she had seen stepping into the house appeared beneath the threshold. "Now, do you believe me?"

In the backlight of the great room, the young woman was even prettier than Maxine had thought. Her golden-blonde hair was clipped and styled in a pixie cut. Her eyebrows looked freshly waxed, shaped into perfect arches. Her small eyes were made to appear larger with liner and mascara, and her full lips looked plump and kissable in berry-colored gloss. She wore a tailored blue suit with an apricot-colored blouse, and her big feet were bare, the toenails clipped and painted in the same hue Maxine wore—a year-round red called Not What It Seems.

The young woman wiggled her toes. "I remembered your favorite color. Does it look good on me?" The lusty red gleamed with a come-hither shine.

"Not as good as it does on me." Maxine winked, hoping to squelch the feeling rising in her chest. She could not reconcile this person as Joe. For some inexplicable reason, she would always view her best friend as Patty, not Pat or Patrick, regardless of the gender change. But this person standing before her was Jo, not Joe. The gravity of the situation felt like a fist to the stomach. The love of her life was no longer a man, but a woman.

"Good one. You're always more quick-witted than me." Jo stepped aside, waving Maxine into the house. "Have you eaten?"

She had—a protein bar—but not dinner. "What do you have?"

"Let me see." Jo shut the door and strode across the dining area into the kitchen. She had the same heavy stride, the bare feet plodding against the hardwood, and the same habit of yanking back one door to the refrigerator and dipping her head inside. She stacked a few glass containers on the counter and let the door swing closed. "Looks like leftover rice and green beans and barbeque chicken."

"Sounds good." Maxine took a seat on a barstool at the cooktop island.

"So, what happened to Patty?" Jo scooped out the leftovers onto two plates and put the first plate in the microwave, covered with a paper towel. It was the same movements Joe used to heat up leftovers, but the body was all wrong.

"I don't know." When Maxine thought about the incident, she toggled back and forth between being mobbed to something more insidious, but less sinister— a stroke or a heart attack. She played with the napkin holder, fluffing the tops of the folded paper until they stood upright, like tufts of white hair. A vague fullness built behind her sinuses. "She was taken away by paramedics. But she's not responding to the messages I sent, and I don't have her parents' phone numbers." She dropped her hands into her lap. "I hate not knowing."

"Hmm." Jo leaned against the counter, folding her arms under her breasts, the same way Joe always did. Her nails clicked against her forearm, and her foot tapped at the same time. "That's why it's so important I get this software released as soon as possible. With brain-to-brain, you don't need to know anyone's phone number. You just think of them, and they respond to you."

The microwave beeped. Jo opened the door, grabbed the silicone mitten from the top drawer of the kitchen cabinet, and placed the plate on the island. She placed the second plate into the microwave and grabbed two forks from the silverware drawer. "Here. Start without me."

It was the same phrase Joe always used, urging her to eat first, even in restaurants when she was served before him. She accepted the fork and grabbed a paper napkin from the holder beside her. "So, when can you reapply for

FCC approval?"

"I don't know. Eli's team is working on a bug fix." Jo fiddled with her earlobe, and a clip-on pearl earring fell against the counter. "Oops. These things don't stay put."

"Pierced earrings are better." Maxine fluffed the rice with her fork. "I can take you to the mall and have them pierced."

"Not now. Maybe later." Jo removed the other earring and set the pair next to the napkin holder. She crossed her arms over her chest again. "As I was saying, once the bug is fixed, we can reapply for FCC approval."

Maxine licked a smear of tangy barbecue sauce from her lips. "Don't you have to redo all that beta testing?"

"Yes, and no."

The microwave beeped again, and Jo removed her plate and set it on the counter. She took a seat next to Maxine and speared a green bean.

"What do you mean by yes and no?" Maxine asked.

Jo stood, strode over to the kitchen cabinet, grabbed two glasses, and filled them with tap water. She set one next to Maxine and took a long swallow from the other. "It's complicated."

"Try me."

A shiver of caution rippled down her legs. Maybe this woman wasn't who she'd said she was. Joe confided everything in her since they had started dating a year ago. They had no secrets. Why now?

"I'm torn." Jo set the glass on the counter and crossed her arms under her breasts. "Before I woke up a woman, I was dead set on forgery to push this product through approvals, but I've grown soft since last night. It's like I've developed a conscience."

Maxine nodded.

The Joe she knew had never hesitated to practice the philosophy of *the ends justify the means*, even if the actions were ethically reprehensible. As long as it brought a product to market that benefited consumers and increased profits, he would do whatever was needed. Developing a conscience was not necessarily in his company's best interest.

"Morality isn't good for business."

"Exactly." Jo resumed sitting. "You know, I've always liked that about you—you have a good head for business."

Maxine smiled. "Never lose sight—"

"Of the bottom line." The last phrase was spoken in unison, the voices crescendoing at the same time.

Jo's gaze softened, and she reached for Maxine's hand.

A jolt of panic—*I'm not a lesbian*—zapped across Maxine's mind. She swiped her fingers away, but not before she encountered the cool, smooth touch of Jo's hairless skin. She froze, startled by the texture. Jo, but not Joe, whose rough skin and hairy knuckles and big palm had eclipsed her whole hand.

Jo withdrew her fingers and dipped her chin toward her chest. "You don't want to be with me anymore, do you?"

Doubt slid across her shoulders, and she stared at her half-eaten plate. What could she say?

"It's okay if you want to break up with me," Jo said. "I'd understand."

But if the roles had been reversed, would Joe have broken up with her?

"I'm just scared." Maxine tore the napkin into tiny shreds in her lap. "I'm not attracted to women, but I'm attracted to you."

"I know. It's confusing." Jo pushed her plate aside and

folded her arms on the counter. "I feel the same way. Not to mention the other things I'm feeling. It's like I don't know who I am anymore. This body feels different. Even my thoughts aren't the same."

"It's the hormones," Maxine said. "Plus, you're on your period. Everything is heightened. My advice is to not make any major decisions until the bleeding stops. You'll feel normal again."

Jo chuckled. "You mean, I'll feel like a man again?"

"No." Maxine shook her head. "You'll just feel better than you do right now."

A long moment of silence stretched between them.

"What do we do now?" Jo asked.

Maxine shrugged. "What do you want to do?"

Jo met her gaze. "I'd like a hug."

"I can do that." Maxine slipped off the stool and opened her arms.

Jo stepped into her embrace, pressing Maxine's face between her breasts.

Maxine turned her head to the side and wrapped her arms around Jo's back and squeezed as tight as she could. The body she held felt soft in all the places that had once felt hard, and she closed her eyes, breathing in the floral scent of Jo's perfume or deodorant, already missing the musky scent of Joe's cologne and woodsy fragrance of his antiperspirant. The pressure in her sinuses finally ruptured, and her eyes leaked with tears. Her body shuddered in spasms, and she felt Jo's arms tighten and her body sway, until they were rocking from side to side—two women in an awkward dancing lullaby. The absurdity of the situation dawned on Maxine, and she chuckled, one rippling laugh punctuating the tears.

"What's so funny?" Jo asked, releasing her.

With the back of her hand, Maxine wiped the tears from her cheeks. "Us." She waved a hand between them. "We're an odd couple."

"As long as we're a couple, I don't care that we're odd." Jo tilted her head. "Do you?"

Full of questions without answers, Maxine shrugged. Her gaze skittered away, and she noticed the clock on the oven read eleven forty-five. "I have to go." She grabbed her backpack and said good night.

"Will I see you again?" Jo asked at the front door.

Maxine searched her face for any signs of Joe. He must still be there, a hint of masculinity, but the longer she looked, the more femininity she saw—from the smooth forehead to the adorned eyes to the hairless cheeks to the glossy lips and smooth chin. She took a step closer and raised on tiptoe to peck Jo's lips. A familiar heat scorched her face, and she fell back on her heels. It was the first time she had kissed a woman. But she hadn't kissed a woman; she had kissed Joe.

She smiled and hoisted her backpack high against her shoulders. "I'll see you tomorrow." She stepped into the cool night.

"Let me know if you hear from Patty."

With a glance over her shoulder, she caught Jo's concerned look beneath the porch light. It was the expression someone gave to a loved one. And although Patty was more Maxine's friend than Jo's friend, they had both known and liked her before and after the switch.

"I will."

CHAPTER 4

"You're cutting it close, missy."

A surge of anger flared in the pit of Maxine's stomach at the sound of her mother's irate voice. She clicked the front door closed and checked the time on her phone. Eleven fifty-five. Didn't her mother sleep? Or did she just lie awake on the sofa, waiting to pounce?

"I'm home before curfew."

She was the only adult she knew who had to be home before midnight. Rules were rules. How could she complain when she wasn't paying rent?

The floorboards creaked in the living room, and the shadow of her mother's stooped body appeared in the hallway. She flicked on the light, and the tunnel of darkness disappeared. She wasn't an old woman, but she acted like one—all aches and pains and hunched shoulders.

"Where were you?"

"Seeing Jo."

"Hmph." Her mother pursed her lips. "I thought you might be at Patty's house, consoling her parents."

Maxine widened her eyes. "Why?"

"I thought you knew." Her mother shifted her stance,

balancing her weight back and forth between her heels.

Maxine recognized her mother's anxious dance. It was the same set of movements she had made when her father died years ago. Every muscle in Maxine's body contracted, but she refused to give in to fear without having any facts.

"Knew what?" She hated playing her mother's game, asking twenty questions to extract the information most people would willingly volunteer all at once.

Her mother paused for dramatic effect, delaying her response to heighten the suspense. "Patty died."

Maxine let the backpack slip from her shoulders, and the backpack collapsed on the floor. *Patty died.* "How?"

"That demonstration mobbed her."

"She died from the stampeding?" All those feet, trampling her best friend.

"No, heart attack." Her mother waved to the living room. "It's on the news."

Maxine dragged her backpack down the hallway and into the living room, where the news played twenty-four/seven on one of the few channels her mother watched. She slumped on the chair next to the sofa, where her mother sat by a table light. With her gaze trained on the moving images, she waited while her mother rewound the video to the announcement.

"Patty Devonshire, a twenty-two-year-old college student, died today during protests at Sonoma State University in Rohnert Park, California. She was part of a movement called The Revolution—a student-led organization, designed to bring pressure to college administrators to support research for a cure for the curious phenomenon that causes some people to switch genders and ages. Paramedics at the scene tried to resuscitate Devonshire, but she was pronounced dead upon arrival at Memorial Hospital. Doctors stated the cause of death was a heart attack. Devonshire had recently been a victim of what medical experts have termed 'spontaneous gender and age reassignment.' She died, inhabiting the body of an eighty-year-old man. Her parents have been contacted, but have refused to give a statement."

Maxine glanced away from the before and after photos of Patty shown on the TV. She rubbed her forehead, trying to stave off a budding headache. No wonder Patty never responded to her texts. No wonder her parents' landline was busy. Tears blurred her vision. She needed to call Jo.

Her mother clicked off the TV. "That college is infecting everyone. You should drop out."

Maxine blinked, and a tear rolled down her cheek. "But I'm only weeks away from graduating."

"What good is graduating as an old man?" Her mother's lips trembled. "No one will hire you."

"No one is hiring me right now, and I'm a young woman." She rubbed the tear off her face and thought of all the job interviews she had declined because they were all in the tech industry. Anger flared in her chest.

"You should stay home. Protect yourself."

Her mother had not worked since Maxine's father had died. She lived off the life insurance policy he'd left her. That was seven years ago. Maxine envisioned spending her days here, with her mother, without the funds to leave or travel.

"How can you be so sure I'll be safe here?" Maxine waved a hand around the room. "What if it's in the air?"

"It's not," her mother said. "Or I would have caught

it already." She hunched forward conspiratorially. "Just between us, I think it's spread sexually."

"Sexually?"

She nodded. "That's why there's all that gender-swapping. It's like when you have kids and you get your DNA all mixed up with your partner and your baby."

Maxine didn't want to refute her mother's argument about the principles of reproduction, so she kept her mouth shut. Rising, she grabbed her backpack and kissed her mother on the top of the head. "I'm tired. I'm going to bed."

Once upstairs, she closed her bedroom door and perched on the edge of the mattress. She called Jo, who answered on the first ring.

"Hey, what's up?"

Maxine listened to the squeaky voice and choked back another impulse to cry. First, Joe had become Jo. Now, Patty was no longer. And her mother wanted her to quit school and stay home.

She swallowed, trying to get the words out without a sob. "Patty died."

"Oh no." Jo inhaled sharply. "Do you need me to come over?"

"It's too late. My mom won't let you come inside."

"You could sneak out and spend the night here."

She groaned, imagining the repercussions of her mother discovering her missing. "I can't."

"What can I do to help?"

"I don't know."

Maxine glanced out the window into the backyard. The sky was dark. The night was quiet. The world seemed to be at rest. But she shifted restlessly against the sheets, tucking her feet under her hips. So much had changed in so little time. The headache throbbed between her temples. She would have to take something soon to relieve the pain, but she didn't want to end the call and face the rest of the night alone.

"Let me talk to you until you fall asleep," Jo said.

The offer sounded tempting, but Maxine knew she could never relax from Jo's high-pitched female voice. At least not yet. "Thanks, but you sound exhausted. You need your sleep too."

"I wish I were there to hold you."

Maxine thought back to their hug in the kitchen. The way their bodies had jigsawed together. A weak smile curled her lips, and she stroked her palm against the soft sheet. "Me too," she said, and she meant it.

Maxine fell asleep and dreamed of the first time she had met Joe at the Chamber of Commerce last year. She was trying to network to get a summer job. She didn't want to work retail, fast food, or temp at an agency where she would be sent wherever needed. She wanted a foothold in the business community, preferably something in tech, in Telecom Valley, something exciting, if unstable. Cutting edge. Daring. Full of potential. Riddled with potholes. Nothing safe.

Even in her dream, she was tiny.

Half-Pint was what the kids had called her while growing up. A plain carton of milk. Growing up hadn't changed anything. She never bothered with makeup. Too costly. The one dress suit she owned was a little too vintage—shoulder pads and knee-length skirt—but her nails were clipped, her hair was straightened, and her skin smelled like the coconut body lotion she used after a bath.

She stumbled into the crowd, weaving her way to the refreshment table, when she overheard a conversation about neuroscientific communication. She had just read something about the topic last semester in a science class, and she interjected an opinion. In the dream, she couldn't remember what she'd said, but the tall, thin man in the haggard suit—who looked like he had come straight from working a twelve-hour day and was in desperate need of a shower, shave, change of clothes, and something to eat that wasn't finger food—pivoted at her comment.

"I'm Joe," he said. His blue eyes pinned her to the floor. "And you are?"

"Maxine." She returned the firm handshake and slid into the rest of the conversation.

She learned he was not an overworked, middle-aged programmer, but the president and CEO of his own telecommunications company, which was developing brain-to-brain communication—a form of telepathy that didn't require implants or the use of cell phones. She had hit the jackpot. She had assumed only job seekers, headhunters, and HR staff from companies scouting for fresh talent attended these events—not anyone from the C-suite. Joe gave her his card and asked her to call him. Before she could secure an entry-level position at his company, she accepted a date and ended up as his girlfriend rather than his employee.

But in the dream, instead of handing her his card, he offered her a kiss. When their lips met, he turned into a woman, and Maxine startled awake, clutching her pillow. She gasped, staring at the shadows on the ceiling. After releasing her grip on the drool-stained pillow, she touched her face to confirm it was still smooth, then squeezed her breasts to confirm they were still soft, then patted between her legs to confirm nothing extraneous dangled there. Only then could she relax her breath into a steady rhythm and feel her temperature return to normal. She was the same person in the same body, and right now, that was the only thing that mattered.

CHAPTER 5

"**W**here you going?"

Maxine startled on the staircase. She must have stepped on the squeaky joist, the one she usually missed, because she hadn't slept well last night. Between the dreams and the worries, she might have totaled four hours of rest. But her mother's question jolted her awake, and she shifted the backpack between her shoulders.

"I'm leaving for school."

Her mother stood at the bottom of the staircase. "School's been canceled. It's all over the news."

A sourness flooded her mouth, and she swallowed the bile in her throat. *Canceled? Over what? The protests?*

"I need to get out." The truth was, Maxine wanted to see Jo before she left for work. She needed a hug, something firm and reassuring, after learning about Patty's death last night.

"Stay home. Protect yourself."

Maxine regretted the decision to live at home so she could finish college in four years instead of working full-time, living on her own, and taking six or seven years to finish. Being a practical person, she didn't dwell on what-ifs. She understood the consequences of her decision, even if she didn't like them.

"Can't I confirm my classes have been canceled? I can't take your word for it."

"Fine, come here and see for yourself. It's all over the news." Her mother moved away from the staircase and shuffled back into the living room.

Maxine followed, placing her backpack on the floor and taking a seat in the chair.

Her mother slouched on the sofa and turned up the volume on the TV. A blanket was crumpled at one end of the sofa and a pillow at the other. A mug of tea sat on the coffee table, along with a half-eaten store-bought muffin on a plate. The living room had become her mother's dwelling place.

After a commercial break, a newscaster said, "Sonoma State University has closed its campus for the rest of the school year. Classes will be held online, including finals and the graduation ceremony. Students are advised to email the university with any questions."

Her mother gave her a sharp look, huffed, and pointed at the screen. "See? It's real. As real as you and me."

Maxine nodded. She had no excuse to leave. At least not right now while her mother was being unreasonable. Maybe later, after online classes and making her mother dinner, Maxine might find a way to cajole her mother into allowing Maxine to leave the house for an hour or two. With that plan in mind, she gathered her backpack and rose, climbing the stairs to her room.

As soon as she closed her bedroom door, Maxine tossed her backpack on her chair and sat on the bed to call Jo. It was only six thirty. Jo usually left work at seven to endure the hour-long commute. The phone rang several times before clicking over to voice mail.

"I need to see you. Please call me."

Maxine ended the call and stared out the window. The sun hadn't reached the roofline, so the backyard was dark, shrouded in shadows. Even the faint outline of the nearly full moon hovered in the sky. The illusion of night in the advent of dawn messed with her mind, and she sent a thought-to-text, hoping to reach Jo as soon as possible.

—*Call me.*—

She sat, watching as the sunlight crested the rooftop and landed squarely in the patch of grass in the backyard, blotting out the shadows, erasing the impression of the moon, and extinguishing all hope of hearing from her beloved.

By lunchtime, Maxine had logged out of her first class and descended the stairs to make her first meal. She had skipped breakfast, not wanting to deal with her mother, and her stomach pinched with pain.

In the kitchen, she made two sandwiches—roast beef and tomato on sourdough bread for her mother and turkey and lettuce on whole wheat for herself—and brought the plates into the living room and set them on the coffee table.

Her mother hunched in the same robe she had worn last night, the belt cinched around her thick waist. When she noticed the sandwiches, she smiled and thanked her daughter.

Maxine nodded, acknowledging the gratitude. She took her accustomed seat in the chair adjacent to the sofa and listened to a panel of two men and two women discuss the rioting that had erupted all over the nation as a record number of college-aged women had turned into elderly men overnight.

"What's happening? Why aren't the men affected?" one hostess asked.

"It's discrimination," another hostess said. "A plot from the patriarchy to do away with women."

"But what about reproduction?" one host asked. "The technology doesn't exist to reproduce without women."

The hostesses laughed.

One hostess leaned forward and placed her elbows on her knees. "You mean there's no one to carry the fetus to term because men's bodies won't accommodate it."

The other hostess wagged a finger in the air. "Implant a uterus. It's been done before. A guy carried to term and delivered the baby by C-section."

The two hosts grimaced.

Maxine fiddled with the crusts on her sandwich. "Can we watch something else?"

While chewing, her mother handed her the remote.

Each channel was nothing but the same. Everyone was talking about the young women turning into old men. Finally, after scrolling through a hundred channels, Maxine landed on something different—the broadcasters were talking about older men waking up as younger women.

"It's affecting Congress," one of the broadcasters said.

"And every other industry dominated by middle-aged males," the other broadcaster said.

The first broadcaster frowned. "It's even affected me." She choked down a cry. "My husband woke up as a woman. I thought someone had played a cruel joke on me. But it was him. He even has the same birthmark on his upper thigh. But everything else is different." She broke down and sobbed, and the camera cut to a commercial.

Maxine turned off the TV.

"Why you do that?" Her mother wagged her fingers. "I wanted to see what happened to her husband. Maybe they'll have before and after photos."

Her mother's voyeuristic pleasure over other people's suffering embarrassed Maxine. She gripped the remote tighter, wondering if she could just remove the batteries or destroy the TV.

A sour taste filled her mouth. Maxine placed her uneaten sandwich on the coffee table and zombie-walked out of the room.

"Come back with the remote."

Maxine didn't listen. She removed the batteries and stashed them in her pocket. From the top drawer in the first kitchen cabinet, she tucked an unopened package of batteries into her other pocket.

"Where you going?" Her mother loomed in the doorway. "You haven't eaten your lunch."

"I'm not hungry."

Her stomach growled, betraying her.

"Give me the remote and go finish your lunch." Frowning, her mother held out her hand.

Maxine surrendered the empty remote.

Her mother palmed the weight and checked the battery holder. "Where the batteries?"

From her pocket, Maxine relinquished the used batteries.

"What you have in the other pocket?" Her mother nodded toward the bulge in her pants.

Sighing, Maxine handed over the package of batteries.

"What wrong with you?" Her mother tapped her

skull. "Do you need to see a doctor?"

Shaking her head, Maxine followed her mother back into the living room. She took her seat in the chair, picked up her plate, and bit into the stale bread, moist lettuce, and dry turkey. She needed something to wash it down, so she returned to the kitchen to pour herself a glass of milk. When she was finished, she glanced up and noticed her mother standing beneath the threshold, watching, waiting, worrying.

Maxine nudged her mother aside and returned dutifully to the living room. She drank the glass of cold iced milk in four swallows as the broadcaster shared before and after photos of her husband who had turned into a young woman.

With a sidelong glance, she studied her mother. Maxine's heartbeat ticked like a time bomb in her chest. How long could she keep Jo's transformation a secret?

"When your next class?" her mother asked.

Maxine finished her sandwich and brushed the crumbs from her hands. "One o'clock."

Her mother checked the time in the right corner of the TV screen. "You better get going."

Maxine gathered her plate and glass and dumped them into the kitchen sink.

Safe behind the closed door of her bedroom, she logged in to the next online class. While waiting for the meeting to start, she checked her phone. No messages. Why hadn't Jo returned any of her phone calls or text messages? Had she left her phone at home again? Or had something else—something worse—happened? Her fingers trembled as she dialed Jo's office.

CHAPTER 6

"Jo Capaldi's office."

Maxine welcomed the friendly, familiar female voice. "Heather, it's Maxine," she said, tucking her legs beneath her hips on the mattress. "Is Jo around?"

"Hi, Maxine," Heather said, her tone softening just a little. "He's actually in the office today, but he's busy with meetings. I'll let him know you called when I see him."

He. Maxine bristled. Jo had decided to keep the masculine pronoun. Would she have done the same?

Heather cleared her throat. "I mean *her*. Ugh, it's so hard to say, isn't it?"

Yes, Maxine agreed, it was.

After the call ended, Maxine tapped her phone against her thigh. Who else might have access to Jo? The list of people was short—the neuroscientists, who Maxine didn't know; the HR manager, Chris, who Maxine didn't want to speak with after Chris, who had transitioned before Jo and whom Jo had treated poorly; and Eli, the chief technology officer and product manager of the B2B team.

She scrolled through her Contacts and found Eli's number. Joe had given it to her when they first started dating.

"I spend most of my nights with him at the office," Joe had said. "We're quite a team, he and I, like father and son. I discovered him, you know."

Joe liked to brag to anyone who would listen about how he'd found Eli, a seventeen-year-old prodigy, through a high school biotech competition and scooped him up with a preemptive offer of employment before Stanford or MIT could offer a full scholarship. Ten years later, Eli was still with Joe. Over the years, their business relationship had deepened into a friendship, and Joe often extended his love and support to Eli's family and friends, even paying for his mother's medical bills when she suffered from breast cancer.

Maxine pressed the green button and listened to the phone ring.

"Eli." As usual, he answered the phone without a greeting.

Maxine wasn't sure if Eli was neurodivergent or not, but his mannerisms seemed to point in that direction. He was a burly guy with a scraggly beard who openly stared at attractive women. No matter how many times Joe had tried to redirect him, Eli wouldn't listen. He never updated his wardrobe or trimmed his beard.

"Hopeless," Joe had called him.

"Clueless," Maxine had wanted to add.

"It's me, Maxine."

"Hi, Maxi," Eli said, his voice brightening.

Maxine hated the nickname. The way he pronounced it made it sound like a joke—Maxi, as in maxi pad. "Is Jo around?"

The beat of silence betrayed him.

"May I speak with her?"

"Umm … Jo's in a meeting."

"With you." Maxine uncurled her legs and stood. The blood rushed to her feet, and she danced on her heels until the sensation of pins and needles left her soles.

"She's not—"

"Maxine." Jo's high, squeaky voice was as breathless as if she had run down the hall and yanked the phone out of Eli's hand. "I'm sorry I haven't returned your calls and texts. It's been a zoo here."

"I figured," she said.

Now that she had Jo on the phone, she didn't know what she wanted to say anymore.

"Listen, I have an emergency board meeting in five minutes. I'll text you after I get off work, and you can meet me at my house."

In the background, the instructor for Maxine's next online class spoke. With a quick tap of some keys, she turned off the volume. "My mom doesn't want me leaving the house. She's afraid I'll end up like you and Patty."

"Why don't you move out?"

The words were spoken flippantly, as if it were a viable option Maxine had completely ignored.

Annoyance smoldered in her gut. "I don't have a job."

"You don't need one," Jo said. "Move in with me."

Maxine blinked, unable to process a response.

"We'll talk more about it tonight," Jo said. "Bye, love."

The call ended, leaving Maxine stunned.

For a long while, she stared at the computer monitor, watching her instructor's mouth move without sound. With a click of a few buttons, the volume returned. The sound blared, strong and insistent, a foghorn warning her to pay attention to this information, which would be included in next month's final exam.

After her last class ended at four, Maxine padded downstairs to make an early dinner. While she drained the hot water from the spaghetti in the kitchen sink, her phone pinged with a message. She set the pot with the limp noodles back on the stove, the steam rising against the backsplash, before she swiped her finger across the screen.

—*Leaving work. Dinner at my place?*—

Maxine stared at Jo's message and considered her options—eat with her mother or have her mother eat alone. Either decision required her to find a way to escape her mother's wrath.

—*Can't tonight. Making dinner for Mom. Will come by later. Will text before I leave.*—

She set her phone aside and dumped a jar of tomato sauce into the pot of spaghetti and brought the mixture back to a simmer. Her phone pinged again. Another swipe of her finger revealed a second message from Jo.

—*If you lived here, you'd never have to make dinner for your mom again. I'd cook for you.*—

A warmth spread across her chest. She smiled, remembering the last time someone had cooked dinner for her. Her father had been alive and well. Her mother bustled about in the kitchen, chopping vegetables for a casserole with potatoes and ham. The food wasn't spectacular. No five-star rating or dense nutritional content. But the comfort of having her family around the table—her mother dressed in a clean outfit, the food prepared with love, her father's rough, broad hand holding her fingers as they prayed—brought back memories of what had been missing since her father's death.

"What you making?"

Maxine flipped her phone face down on the counter and stirred the sauce. "Spaghetti. We're out of ground beef. And French bread. But I figured we could butter some toast."

Her mother shuffled over to the stove and peered over her shoulder, sniffing. "Needs more basil and a dash of pepper."

Tension knotted along Maxine's spine. If her mother had the audacity to criticize her cooking without tasting the dish, her mother could eat alone.

"Why don't I run out and get some garlic bread and meatballs? You can man the stove. Add as many spices as you want." She stepped aside and handed the wooden ladle to her mother.

"Why leave? You can place your order on a delivery app."

"They never pick out the right food."

"Then don't pay them."

Maxine gritted her teeth. Her mother still had not accepted the dripping ladle. Maxine glowered at her unkempt hair, knotted like a makeshift bird's nest, and the sour-smelling housecoat. A flare of frustration rose up within her, and she tossed the ladle on the counter, missing the spoon rest. Red sauce splattered like thick blood on the white counter. With a damp sponge, she mopped up the mess. She turned off the heat, covered the pot, and seized her phone from the counter.

"I'm leaving. Enjoy your meal."

"Where you going?" Her mother loomed in the doorway.

Quick, shallow breaths heaved from Maxine's chest,

and her hands balled into fists. "None of your business."

"As long as you live in my house, it is my business."

Jo's offer returned, unbidden, in her mind. But Maxine resisted the siren song. She wanted to make it on her own, not run from her mother's house to her lover's house. Still, the offer was tempting.

"Jo invited me to dinner."

Her mother's face crumpled. "You're so beautiful. You could have anyone."

The tears in her mother's throat brought moisture to Maxine's eyes. When her father had been alive and well, her mother had cherished everything. But once he died, she questioned everything. She had married for love, but the love of her life had died and left her money. Most women would have appreciated a man who provided beyond the grave, but not Maxine's mother. She held it against him. Like he had planned his exit and left her with enough cash so he wouldn't feel guilty for being gone and leaving her alone. Didn't she realize she could date and find love again? But that wasn't who she was or what she wanted. Maxine understood that. Her mother liked to dwell on the negative of a situation. She preferred to worry until she was miserable. She wanted everyone to sympathize with her alleged plight. How dare anyone acknowledge the truth—she was a well-provided-for widow, young enough to love again.

"I have who I want." Maxine punched her fists against her waist. "Why don't you go find someone new?"

"I wouldn't need someone new if your father hadn't left," she said.

"You talk as if he abandoned you when all he did was die."

"Either way, he's gone." Her voice fractured, and she

wagged a finger. "Mark my words. Your Joe will leave you one day. Because he's old."

"He's not old, Mom. He's mature." Her stomach churned with guilt for lying by omission, but she didn't want to explain to her mother that Joe had switched and was now a young woman.

"He's old enough to be your father."

So what if he once had been? Maxine straightened her shoulders. What difference did it make, especially now that she and Joe were the same age, like twin sisters?

The headache from last night returned, and she rubbed her forehead. After dropping her hand, she turned away from her mother to grab a glass from the cabinet and filled it with water from the sink. She took two ibuprofen for the pain and swallowed the pills with gulps of cool water. When she was finished, she placed the glass in the sink and gripped the ledge with both hands, her head downcast, her eyes blinking. If she tried to explain the situation, she would be here for hours.

"I have a plan," Maxine said. She pivoted toward her mother. "You go take a shower and change into some fresh clothes, and I will order garlic bread and meatballs for delivery."

"What about your boyfriend?" Her mother narrowed her gaze.

She shrugged. "He can eat without me."

Her mother stared for a long moment before her face softened. "Okay."

As soon as Maxine heard the water plunk through the pipes upstairs, she opened an app on her phone and placed her order. While she waited, she set the dining room table. By the time her mother descended the stairs, dressed in a clean T-shirt and slacks with an elastic waistband, the food had arrived. Fresh meatballs and warm garlic bread from the local deli. Maxine ladled the spaghetti onto the plates, topped each with a generous serving of meatballs, cut the garlic bread into thick wedges, and placed them on bread plates. She filled glasses with water and placed a white napkin on her mother's lap.

After taking a seat across from her mother, she lifted her water glass for a toast. "To family."

Her mother clinked her glass against hers. "I'll drink to that."

A bottomless pit of hunger opened in Maxine, and no amount of spaghetti and meatballs and garlic bread she ate could fill that darkness. How would she escape? Not just tonight to see Jo. But forever. Not by moving from her mother's house to Jo's house, but by moving into her own place, paying her own bills, creating her own life. The original plan to stay home, focus on school, and graduate within four years now seemed ridiculous. She should have done what her classmates had done—worked part-time, moved out with roommates, and cobbled together some makeshift form of independence. Now it was too late.

She grasped her fork so tightly that her hand cramped. She flexed and curled her fingers, drank some more water, and picked up the fork again. Maybe she should have accepted those interviews with Joe's competition. No one else wanted to hire her. A pressure built behind her sternum. Assuming the pain was nothing but heartburn, she declined seconds and rose to package the leftovers.

After the kitchen was cleaned, she offered to go upstairs with her mother and crawl into her mother's bed to watch a movie.

"Like old times," she said, meaning before her father died.

Her mother agreed, and the two of them turned off the lights and ascended the stairs to the front of the house, where her mother's room overlooked the street. Maxine pulled the blackout curtains her father had bought and turned on the TV. Her mother climbed into bed and burrowed underneath the covers. Maxine snuggled beside her, flipping through the channels until she landed on something familiar. A comedy about neighbors. Something benign and meaningless and full of laughter. Something light to take their minds off the circumstances that surrounded them.

Halfway through the movie, Maxine heard a rhythmic snore. Her mother slept with her head tilted back, mouth open, like a dead fish. Maxine set the sleep timer on the TV for thirty minutes, slipped out of bed, and turned off the light. She tiptoed down the stairs with her backpack nestled between her shoulder blades.

Exiting through the front door, she shivered at the shock of cold air. She stepped back inside for a moment to grab a jacket from the hall closet. Cocooned in its warmth, she locked the front door and slipped into her car. She sent Jo a thought-to-text to let her know she was on her way. Instead of starting the engine, she shifted into neutral and allowed the tires to roll down the driveway into the street. When another car entered the cul-de-sac, she finally turned the key in the ignition, flicked on the headlights, and sliced through the night.

CHAPTER 7

"There you are." Jo flung open the front door and ushered Maxine inside the warmth of the great room. "I thought you'd never arrive."

"It was hard leaving." Maxine glanced at the clock on the oven. Nine thirty. "I had to watch half a movie with her to get her to sleep."

"Sounds like when I babysit Eli's nephews. Those guys are hard to get down for the night." She shook her head and offered Maxine a seat on the sofa. "So, before I launch into my day, which will take forever to tell you about, tell me what's new with you first."

Maxine didn't have much to say that was different from what she had said before about her strenuous relationship with her mother, her lack of financial resources, and her desire for independence—and the terror of what her mother would do or say once she discovered Jo was now a woman.

"Tell me about it," Jo said, pressing her legs together—which, by habit, kept springing apart. Finally, she sighed and crossed her legs with one ankle over the knee. The soft material of her athleisure brushed against Maxine's thigh.

Maxine stiffened from the light touch. A frisson

of energy powered up her leg and warmed her lap. She swallowed and glanced away, not knowing how to process the curious sensation.

She had never been attracted to women. Not even during that experimental phase in high school when her girlfriends had often practiced French-kissing each other in preparation for their first kiss with a boy. She declined the offers, saying she would risk looking inexperienced. Her girlfriends giggled, thinking she was insane. But the thought of her tongue probing another woman's mouth had dried up all thoughts of romance.

Now she found the opposite to be the case. Her whole body seemed to flower for more of Jo's physical attention. But that, she reasoned, was because Jo was really Joe, and the desire for her to return to a male lingered in the background, like constant white noise. She reached out and grazed her fingertips across Jo's wrist.

Jo grabbed her hand and entwined their fingers. "When I walked into the office, no one recognized me," she said. "Thank God Chris was around. He understood everything. Though he wasn't kind at first." She pursed her lips and glanced away for a moment. A sadness lingered in her expression, something Maxine recognized from when she had been Joe, but the look was fleeting. Jo's attention flickered back to Maxine's face, and she continued with her story. "Anyway, by the time the company-wide announcement was made, the board of directors called an emergency meeting." With her other hand, she tapped Maxine's thigh. "Can you believe they wanted to fire me? Because I'm young now and a woman. Talk about discrimination. I had to get Chris involved again. It was a mess."

Maxine nodded. She didn't want to mention how

discriminatory Jo had been when she was a man, refusing to hire female neuroscientists and biotech engineers in favor of male talent. The hypocrisy brought a sour taste to her mouth, and she swallowed down the bile in her throat.

"Anyway," Jo said, "I got everything straightened out for now, including a new round of beta testing. We have an agreement with the FCC for expeditated approval if we can document thirty thousand error-free transmissions with the software updates." She pulled a thumb drive from a pocket and waved it like a victory flag. "I thought we could install it and try it out tonight. Just for fun."

For fun? From what Maxine knew, Jo never did anything "for fun."

She straightened her spine and extracted her fingers from Jo's hand. "Let me get this straight. You want us to install the software into our brains and not have it count toward the thirty thousand transmissions needed for FCC approval?"

Nodding, Jo tried to grab her hand again.

Maxine curled her fingers into a fist. "I don't want to be a guinea pig unless my experience counts."

"Oh, baby, your experience matters. I just can't document it because you're not employed by my company and you're not one of the original test subjects." Jo pouted. "The FCC has strict guidelines we must follow."

The old Joe wouldn't have cared about those guidelines. He would have cut corners, skip steps, even lied if necessary. He had been a ruthless businessman, always eyeing the bottom line, and that was who Maxine was comfortable dealing with and loving. This new Jo, with her inclusionary vision—from offering her a peripheral spot in the beta testing to asking her to move into her home—shook the bedrock of their relationship, challenging Maxine in ways she'd never imagined.

Jo seemed to sense her resistance. She uncurled her legs and stood, pacing around the coffee table, just like Joe would do. "I understand your concerns. I did my best in the past to keep you at arm's length from my company —both for the health of our relationship and the well-being of my corporation. But everything's changed." She sat on the edge of the sofa, hands clenched in a desperate knot between her thighs, and leaned so close to Maxine that she could see the pores on her face. "I want you in all aspects of my life. Not shoved into a cubicle of my existence, like you have been. But included everywhere with everything." She sprang her hands loose, leaning back and spreading her arms wide to demonstrate the enormity of her proposition.

Panic lurched in Maxine's chest, and her pulse quickened to double time. Sweat poured into the palms of her hands, and she wiped them down on her jeans. The prospect of being everything to the one person she had hoped would give her the opportunity of gainful employment suddenly soured her stomach. Over the past ten months, the mutual camaraderie of a shared vision and similar values had slowly evolved into love. Trusting her instincts, she'd learned to relax into their May-December romance, even fighting against her mother to maintain the connection, but this newness of Joe becoming Jo—not just physically, but emotionally— dismantled the established order between them. If she allowed it to continue, she feared it would unhinge the rest of her life in ways she never imagined.

"I can't."

Frowning, Jo settled back against the sofa cushions.

"No, you can. It's that you won't." She folded her arms across her breasts. "It's because I'm a young woman, right? That's what it boils down to now. Whenever something goes wrong or I can't get something right, it's because I'm young and a woman."

"That's not what I'm saying." Maxine ran her fingers through her hair and gathered the strands into a makeshift ponytail, which she tossed over one shoulder. "It's too much, all at once, and you know it." She ticked off the reasons on her fingers. "One, you wake up a woman. Now, my boyfriend is a girlfriend, and I'm not gay. What do I do? Two, you ask me to move in with you. You've never asked before, not even when I brought it up months ago after a fight with my mother. You just looked at me gravely and nodded your head and said, 'You're smart. You'll figure it out.' Now you extend the invitation like it's no big deal. How am I supposed to react? And three." She paused, catching her breath and her focus. "You ask me to install the software to test for fun instead of allowing me to be a part of the official study. Like we're two kids on the playground and not two adults experimenting with mind-altering software. Why am I not to object?" She threw her hands down on her lap. "I don't know you anymore."

Jo puckered her lips, her eyes filling with moisture. "Is this how you felt when Patty switched?" Her voice warbled, and a tear streaked down her face.

Sighing, Maxine rubbed her forehead. That damn headache had returned. Would it ever leave her? She closed her eyes for a moment, trying to regain her thoughts, trying to rewind the memories. She circled back to the moment when Patty had called her in the middle of the night to say she had gotten up to go to the bathroom and discovered she had a penis. The strange, croaking voice penetrated the fog of her sleepy mind, and she remembered how she'd hugged her legs to her chest, the phone pinned against one ear, the sound of her blood rushing louder than the words Patty spoke.

"No," Maxine said, "that's not how I felt." She scrubbed her face with both hands and widened her eyes. "I felt protective of Patty. We were the same age. We grew up together. When she became an old man, all I could think about was how I could keep her as my best friend." She inhaled sharply, clutching her chest with a tight fist, hoping to stanch the feelings rising within her. "But she was so set on stopping everything by joining The Revolution, and I know her thinking was faulty, but she was desperate. And now she's dead. If she hadn't been protesting, she wouldn't have been in that stampede, and maybe, just maybe, her heart would have lasted a little bit longer." Her voice broke.

Jo reached for her hand, and Maxine allowed for the comfort. "I'm sorry, baby. I didn't mean to upset you."

Nodding, Maxine scooted closer. She buried her face against Jo's shoulder and cried big, wet, sloppy tears. She allowed Jo to envelop her in a warm embrace. For a while, being in Jo's arms felt like being with her mother, all softness. But the way Jo stroked her hair was the same way Joe had, one long paw from scalp to back, and arousal took over—that undeniable sexual longing that had bound them together when they were opposite genders and which continued to bind them in a curious way that neither one could understand or explain.

"We don't need to install the software," Jo whispered into her ear.

And just as she said those words, Maxine felt her

resistance fall away. "But if we do, then we can be in touch instantly, anytime and anywhere, right?"

"That's right." Jo placed a soft kiss against her forehead.

Maxine sighed and relaxed further. She ran her lips across Jo's collarbone. "Okay."

"Okay, what?" Jo nibbled on her earlobe.

A ripple of pleasure danced across her skin, and Maxine skipped her tongue up the length of Jo's neck until she caught her lips with her mouth.

Excitement spread throughout her body, and she broke free for only a moment to say, "Let's install the software," before her mouth collapsed against Jo's mouth, stifling the low moan that emitted between Jo's lips.

Afterward, at the comfort of the dining room table, where Jo worked, even though she had an office in an empty bedroom, Maxine sat on a chair and adjusted the earbuds.

Jo hunched over her laptop to begin the installation of the proprietary software. "I had it done at the lab today. It takes sixty seconds to download, but overnight to install. You won't feel anything. But you might hear some sounds."

Nodding, Maxine closed her eyes and waited. A series of clicks and whirs emitted through the earbuds. It reminded her of how her father had described the MRI machine that scanned his brain for tumors. She listened until the sounds ended.

"The download's complete," Jo said.

Blinking, Maxine removed the earbuds and glanced around the table at the papers Jo had brought home from the office. She didn't feel any differently. The headache that throbbed beneath her forehead still lingered, but the sensation had dulled into something tolerable.

"Go home and get some sleep," Jo said, "and we'll test it in the morning when you wake up." She shut down her laptop, stood, and offered Maxine a hand.

Taking Jo's warm fingers, Maxine pushed back from the table and stood. Her legs supported her body. No side effects of dizziness, like Jo had experienced earlier in the day. No, she felt fine. Stable, clearheaded, awake. Better than she had anticipated.

At the front door, Jo helped her slip back into her coat.

Maxine adjusted her backpack between her shoulders. "So, tomorrow morning, you'll contact me by phone or thought?"

"By thought," Jo said. "I'll ask to engage with you, and once you accept, we can have a conversation."

"And if I don't want to talk?"

"You don't accept the engagement."

"How?"

"You'll see tomorrow. It's not as hard as I'm making it sound."

Maxine wondered if Jo's engagement would wake her from a deep sleep or if the software only worked while you were awake. But she didn't ask. She stretched up on her tiptoes and threw her arms around Jo's neck and planted a kiss on her soft lips. For a moment, she imagined not going. What would her life look like if she decided to stay, move in, and call this place home? No more blaring TV talk shows. No more obligatory meals with her mother. No more questions about where she was going, who she was seeing, or what she was doing with her time. Just moments like this, with Jo's tongue exploring her mouth, her soft hands slipping beneath her T-shirt.

With a groan, Jo broke off the kiss and dropped her hands from Maxine's back. "I'm sorry. But if we keep doing this, I won't let you leave."

Maxine fell back on her heels. "I understand." The vision of her life here ended with the kiss.

She opened the front door, and a brisk chill swept into the house. She shivered, running down the lighted pathway to her car, where she slipped inside and started the engine. She powered up the heater, rubbing her hands before the vents until the blood pulsed in her fingertips. She glanced at the house one last time and glimpsed Jo standing at the window, her face pressed against the glass. A longing all out of proportion swelled within Maxine. All she had to do was turn off the engine, exit the car, and walk up the path. Jo would open the door and welcome her back inside. She would lace her fingers together with Jo's and follow her to the back of the house to what would become their bedroom. She could lie down and forget about everything that had happened since her father had died.

Jo waved and dropped the curtain.

The window closed its sleepy eye.

Next, the lights flicked off.

The house was dark in slumber.

One moment of hesitation was all it took for a decision to be made. Patty's joining The Revolution. Her father's diagnosis and failed treatment. Her mother buying into conspiracy theories. Her fear of never making it on her own.

For a long moment, Maxine gazed at the empty street, listening to the anxious tick of her pulse echoing in her ears. Somewhere inside her brain, the software sat, waiting for her to fall asleep so it could begin the installation process. She gripped the steering wheel, the engine purring, the car still parked outside Jo's house.

A flicker of doubt passed through Maxine's mind. Was it too late to back out? The download had taken only sixty seconds, but the process to remove the software would require a trip to the lab. A neuroscientist would have to locate the software and erase that part of her mind. What would happen if too much or too little was deleted? Jo had reassured her the procedure was safe if she chose to have the software uninstalled, but Maxine couldn't help but wonder what if a memory she cherished was erased or some information she needed for a final exam was deleted?

Stop worrying. You're becoming your mother.

She steeled her mind and shifted into drive. Pulling away from the curb, she decided to trust Jo, trust the software, and trust her decision to believe in the power of science, for her faith in God had failed. No number of prayers could bring back her father, just like no number of prayers could bring back Patty. The only things that existed lay before her—the empty streets, the full moon, and the unseasonably cold spring air.

CHAPTER 8

Maxine?

Maxine jerked awake in her twin-size bed. The pink walls of her childhood bedroom surrounded her. She blinked several times, trying to focus through the remnants of sleep.

A robotic voice crackled through her mind. *Do you accept this transmission?*

Yes, Maxine thought, *I do.*

A click and whir buzzed and hummed as her mind connected with Jo's mind. The sensation prickled across her scalp like tiny needles before the vibration disappeared, and a space opened in her mind.

Good morning, baby. How did you sleep?

Jo's thoughts sounded just like her voice—confident and a little squeaky.

Okay, but I could use some more. Maxine wondered how she sounded. Sleepy or annoyed?

She rolled over on the narrow mattress, and her body ached. Last night, to avoid waking her mother, she had climbed the lattice, woven with ivy, that trailed up the side of the house and snuck into her bedroom window. It was a stunt she used to pull during high school when her parents refused to let her go out after ten—the time most teenage parties started. The climb was usually swift and uneventful, but last night, she had struggled with her grip on the wooden slats. The muscles in her arms burned, and her thighs twitched from the effort. Now she felt black and blue all over. A quick glance confirmed her body was intact. No markings whatsoever. Still, she went through her daily ritual, patting her face (smooth), cupping her breasts (full), and touching between her legs (empty) before relaxing against the pillow.

What time is it?

Time for me to get ready for work. Big day ahead.

She rolled onto her side, almost expecting to see Jo's face lying beside her—the voice was so clear, so crisp, so real. She stroked her hand against her pillow and smiled.

I love you, she thought.

Love you more. Talk later.

The robotic voice returned. *Disengaged.*

The silence that filled her mind was as loud as a vacuum. Her scalp prickled again. Once the sensation ended, her mind cleared, like a bank of fog lifted, exposing the familiar terrain of regular thoughts that flitted back and forth like butterflies landing on flowers. She swung her legs over the mattress and padded down the hallway to shower and change.

When she descended the stairs a half hour later, she heard the TV in the living room. She stepped beneath the threshold and smiled at her mother, who sat on the sofa in her ratty robe and slippers, sipping from a mug of coffee.

"I enjoyed that movie last night. We should do that more often."

"Yeah, I agree," Maxine said. "But not tonight. I have class till ten."

Her mother shuffled some papers on the coffee table. "Patty's mom called while you were in the shower. We've been invited to the funeral on Saturday. I told her we would go."

Maxine twirled a strand of hair around her finger and pursed her lips. "Why do you want to go?"

Rarely, her mother left the house.

"Seems the right thing to do. They paid their respects when your father died."

They had. Maxine inhaled deeply and released the tight coil of hair, which spun free and fanned against her shoulder. It was dark brown, like her father's had been when he was younger. She wondered if she would go gray and bald like him when she was older. Like Patty had, looking like her grandfather.

She shuddered and shook her head, hoping to dislodge the negative thoughts that seemed to gather like storm clouds in her mind. "I guess we'll go."

"I'll drive," her mother said.

Her mother seldom drove. She preferred to pay extra for the stores to deliver to her front door.

"I don't want you driving while crying," her mother said. "I know you two were close."

"Okay." Maxine said the word even though an uneasiness squeezed her chest. "Would you like me to make us breakfast before I log in to my first class?"

Her mother smiled from her lips to her eyes. "Yes, that would be wonderful. I just love your cinnamon toast."

Maxine padded into the kitchen; poured herself a mug of coffee, sweetened with creamer; then began making her mother's favorite cinnamon toast. Halfway through the process, she forgot how much cinnamon to use and how much butter. She forgot which cupboard housed the sugar and which one housed the plates. What was happening? Was the software making her senile?

Engage Jo.

After the robotic voice confirmed Jo would receive the transmission, Maxine thought, *Hey, I know you have a busy morning, but I'm concerned. I'm having some memory problems. Is this a side effect of the software?*

No, it shouldn't be. None of the beta tests showed any signs of memory issues.

Maxine glanced out the window at her car parked along the curb, where she'd left it last night. That headache she had been fighting for the past few days seemed to have finally receded.

Okay. Just checking. Maybe it's just stress. I have finals in three weeks, and I don't know if I'm ready.

You're smart. You'll be ready.

How are things with you?

Just peachy. Pulling into the parking lot. Will think with you later. Okay?

Maxine could hear the concern in Jo's voice. She promised not to worry. *Okay.*

The robotic voice returned. *Disengaged.*

With the toast ready, Maxine set a plate on a TV tray and brought it to her mother. She returned a few moments later with her own plate and mug of coffee and sank into the chair beside her. Watching the newscaster talk about the weather, explaining why this week was unseasonably cool for the first week in May, seemed so normal that Maxine almost believed the world had returned to some semblance of order.

On Saturday morning, Maxine opened her closet and

selected the same black dress she had worn to her father's funeral. She draped the towel that had been wrapped around her freshly showered body onto the back of her chair and shimmied into a pair of underwear.

When she bent to hook the bra around her back, her fingers wouldn't cooperate. She paused, rubbing her fingertips over the knuckles, wondering why the joints seemed unusually swollen. Blaming it on the five hours it had taken to type up a paper on economic theory, she massaged lotion into her hands, something she had seen her mother do when her doctor said she had the beginnings of osteoarthritis. The trick worked, and she was able to finally match the hooks and eyes together.

Next, she slipped off the polyester dress from the wooden hanger and tugged the dress over her head. The material fell over her angular body, and she smoothed a hand over her flat stomach.

"Your dad says hi!"

The voice seemed to come from above, not inside her head.

Maxine glanced up, pressing her fingertips to her temples. "Jo?"

"Not Jo, silly."

The voice didn't sound like Jo's. It was an octave lower and deeper.

Maxine glanced around the room from the open closet to the window. "Who are you? Where are you? And how do you know my father?" The questions shot rapid-fire from her mouth.

"It's me, Patty. I'm in heaven. I've known your dad my whole life."

Patty? In heaven?

Sinking to the edge of her mattress, Maxine

concentrated on activating the software to contact Jo.

As soon as the robotic voice confirmed the connection, Maxine thought, *I'm hearing voices other than yours.*

Strange. The only other person who has the software installed right now is Eli.

It's not a male voice. It's female. She says she's Patty in heaven and that my father says hi.

The pause in the transmission allowed for a crackle of feedback.

"It's pretty cool here," said the disembodied voice who claimed to be Patty. "I think you'd like it."

Maxine balled her hands into fists. "I'm not dying anytime soon," she said.

Even from beyond the grave, Patty was pushing an agenda. Maxine wouldn't have any of it.

She stood and searched the closet for her black flats. "I'm happy here. I'm young. I'm healthy."

"Don't be so snippy," Patty said. "I thought you'd like to know I'm okay."

Maxine shifted through the odds and ends on the closet floor. "How come I can't see you?"

"I don't have a body anymore."

Great. I'm being haunted by my best friend.

Maxine unearthed her black flats. As she slipped her feet into the shoes, she received another transmission.

Maxine? Jo's voice penetrated her thoughts.

She strode over to the mirror above the dresser and dragged a brush through her damp hair. *Yes, Jo.*

I think you've encountered a software bug.

No way.

Yes, it's possible. Another company had an FCC violation last year for penetrating the veil between this world and the next. *It's very likely Eli's team broke the barrier when they fixed the other issues.*

Great. Just great. She hoped the sarcasm came through the transmission.

Her frustration showed through her efforts to uncap a tube of lipstick. Her achy fingers fumbled a few times before she dislodged the cap. Leaning closer to the mirror, she smeared a swatch of color across her lips.

How can I stop communicating with Patty in heaven?

I don't know.

Static crackled, and the robotic voice announced the transmission with Jo had disengaged.

"Maxine!" her mother called from the bottom of the staircase. "Are you ready to leave? I don't want to be late."

"I'm coming!" Maxine tossed her phone into her backpack and headed for the stairs.

Her hand clutched the railing, and her feet trembled with each step.

At the bottom of the staircase, her mother scowled. She wore the same black dress she had worn to her husband's funeral with the same black leather shoes. Maxine knew if Patty's funeral hadn't fallen under her mother's definition of "the right thing to do"—along with flying the flag on national holidays, passing out candy on Halloween, and singing carols on Christmas—she would be slumped on the sofa, watching doomsday TV.

Before her foot touched the floor, her mother asked, "What took you so long?"

"I had to iron the dress," Maxine lied.

"Hmph." Her mother shuffled to the garage door. "Who were you talking to?"

Maxine paused. How could she explain what she had just heard without appearing loony? She gulped, swallowing the weird paranoia in the back of her throat. "Um … Jo."

"What did he want?"

Her mother pressed a button, and the garage door lifted. A shaft of golden light cut across the concrete floor and illuminated her lined, worried face.

"He just wanted to say hi."

Maxine slid into the passenger seat of her mother's car. It still had that new-car smell. Her father had purchased the vehicle just months before he died, and her mother rarely drove it. Maxine had once asked if she could have it, but her mother refused. That was how Maxine had ended up with the old sedan she had parked next to her mother's newer one.

"Figures." Her mother huffed before starting the engine. "That man has nothing substantial to say. I don't know why you talk to him every day."

"You and Dad talked every day when you were dating." Maxine twined her fingers together. "I don't see a problem with it."

"Your father and I were the same age." Her mother shifted into reverse and glanced over her shoulder. The car eased down the driveway. Once she pulled into the street, she clicked the garage door closed and shifted into drive. "We had tons in common. You and Joe are so far apart in age; you have nothing to discuss. That's why he calls just to say hi."

Maxine fumed. She was thankful her mother couldn't hear her thoughts.

"Look at that mess up ahead!" Maxine's mother pointed to the sea of red taillights in the near distance.

She leaned into her horn, and the blaring sound was followed by other drivers honking their horns.

Maxine cringed.

"What's the holdup?" Her mother honked again. She strained against the seat belt, trying to locate the distraction.

Peering out the window, Maxine identified the problem. A group of protesters blocked the intersection leading to downtown, including the mayor's office, the hospital, and the funeral home.

So many old men and young women picketed with signs, all screaming the same chant, "Give us back our bodies!"

Sirens blared, and blue lights flashed as police cars wedged through the stopped traffic. Officers parked over curbs and evacuated their vehicles. They were dressed in riot gear. Some of them spoke into megaphones, requesting the group to disband.

"We don't want to arrest anyone," an officer said. "Go quietly. Or we will use force."

Maxine leaned her head against the side window and observed the chaos. With nothing else to do, she started a transmission. *Engage Jo.*

"I don't know why I bothered to get dressed," her mother said, shaking her head. "We'll never get through this mess." She rolled down her window and tried to flag a police officer. "Sir, we need to get through to attend a funeral."

The officer leaned down, and his face was covered with a shield. "I'm sorry, ma'am. The roads are closed because of the protesters. We're not sure when they'll reopen. We have to clear the protesters first. I suggest you turn around and head home before violence breaks out."

"Violence," her mother gasped. "My word, what's the world coming to?"

A staticky crackle filled the air, then …

"What's he talking about?" Patty asked. "My parents paid good money for this funeral. It'd better happen."

Not now, Patty. I'm waiting to hear from someone.

"I know. That boyfriend who's now a woman. Does that make you gay?"

Her mom swiveled, the car engine idling, and asked, "Who are you talking to?"

Maxine frowned. "I didn't say anything."

"Yes, you did. Something about waiting to hear from someone. Maybe you should call Patty's parents. Tell them we can't get through because of the protests. Maybe they can reschedule."

"I don't think you can reschedule a funeral."

"You never know." Her mom nodded toward the phone in Maxine's lap.

I should just send a thought-to-text. This brain-to-brain technology isn't working. She pressed the keys to unlock her phone.

The robotic voice confirmed Jo had been engaged.

Maxine? Jo's voice rattled inside her head. *Sorry for the delay. We were cut off by some interference. I need to talk to Eli on Monday. See what the bug is all about.*

A flare of indignation heated Maxine's face. *But he doesn't know I have the software installed.*

She steeled her mind, willing herself not to think about the things she felt. But the thoughts flew across her mind before she could contain them. *This is why I wanted to be part of the authorized study.* She inhaled deeply. *I wanted these types of things documented and resolved.*

She might be young, but she did possess a heavy dose

of reason. Why Jo never bothered to listen to her, she would never know.

Don't worry. I'll tell him these voices are happening to me.

She held her breath, tapping her nails against the back of her phone. *Okay.* She instructed the software to disengage.

As soon as she heard the robotic voice's confirmation, she blew out her breath, flipped the phone over, and dialed the landline for Patty's parents. The phone rang several times before clicking over to voice mail. She left a brief message.

"No one's home," she told her mother. She glanced out the window at the stalled traffic. "I don't have her parents' cell numbers. Do you?"

Her mother shook her head. "I think I left it on the coffee table. I didn't think we'd need it."

At the nearest intersection, an officer redirected traffic to a side street.

Her mother followed the officer's directions, steering away from the mob of protesters.

The air crackled.

"Oh well," Patty said. "It was going to be a closed casket anyway."

Maxine rubbed her temples, wishing the cacophony of voices would go away. She didn't have the ability to carry on simultaneous conversations.

"You okay?" her mother asked at a four-way stop. "You look sick."

"I'm fine," Maxine lied.

"You don't look fine. You need to go lie down when we get home."

Maxine tipped her head back against the seat rest. She

watched the traffic snaking along the back roads. The car inched forward.

Her mother patted Maxine's knee. "I'm sorry we didn't get to say goodbye to your friend."

"No worries." *I'm talking with her right now. She hasn't gone anywhere. Just her body has.*

"Speak up if you're saying something."

A cold shiver rippled down Maxine's spine. She sat upright in the seat and swiveled to glance at her mother. Could she hear her thoughts? "I didn't say anything."

"I swear you were talking." Her mother glowered, hands gripping the steering wheel. "Mumbling like your father used to do. My hearing is good, but not that good. Speak up."

"I wasn't talking." She eyed her mother. *I was thinking. Can you hear my thoughts?*

But her mother didn't answer. Her gaze was fixed on traffic, her attention focused on getting them home.

CHAPTER 9

O n Saturday night, Maxine sat next to her mother, watching the breaking news on TV. The governor issued an emergency statewide curfew. Everyone had to be inside by ten o'clock each night. If you worked at night or commuted, you needed a permit. Police officers would be allowed to pull anyone over at certain checkpoints to verify the drivers had a permit.

"The end is near," her mother said, pulling the quilt over her knees. "I guess that means I'll see more of you at night."

Maxine gulped. When would she see Jo?

Don't worry, child of light. Don't worry.

Maxine glanced up, searching for the voice. It was deep, resonant, and masculine. It almost sounded like—

"Dad?" Maxine whispered his name under her breath. Her heartbeat lurched in her chest. She wiped her palms on the thighs of her jeans.

"It's Mom, dear." Her mother frowned, staring at her. "I think you've been studying too much. Maybe tomorrow, between classes, we could go for a walk around the block and get some fresh air. It's not like there's much to worry about anymore with the end of the world coming."

Maxine bit her lower lip. Her mother never wanted to

walk. Why now? Could she hear her father too?

Don't worry about your mother, her father said. *She only cares about you.*

I know, but she drives me crazy with her conspiracy theories.

That only brings her comfort. Everyone needs something to believe in.

But they're lies. Aren't they?

Don't worry.

Why won't you answer my question?

Don't worry. We'll talk soon.

The voice left the room. Maxine could feel its absence, like when a breeze dies down and the air becomes still.

"I think you're right," Maxine said, standing. "I've been too preoccupied with finishing this last semester and searching for a job. I'll go to sleep early. Get some rest. We can go for a walk tomorrow."

Her mother nodded. "That's sounds like a good plan. I'll be upstairs shortly. I don't need to watch much more of this nonsense."

By the time Maxine had slipped beneath the covers, she heard her mother turn off the TV and pad up the stairs. The creaky floorboards announced her presence in the hallway before the bedroom door clicked shut. Lying against the pillow, with the moonlight streaming through the curtain, Maxine engaged Jo.

When will I see you again? Maxine asked.

I don't know. But we'll figure something out. We always do.

Maxine fiddled with her hands, her fingers clutching and releasing the sheet. *I spoke with my father just now.*

Jo groaned. *It's a bug. I swear it is. Eli's team will have to fix it. I just hope the FCC doesn't find out about the violation.*

The company could be fined, or the project could be shut down.

A sense of peace settled on Maxine's chest. *I wouldn't worry about it. You had similar concerns with thought-to-text, and everything worked out.*

Jo heaved a sigh. *We had problems translating thoughts into text, but we never had problems with transmissions.* Her voice sounded heavy with defeat. *And we never violated any government regulations. I'm afraid once I tell Eli, he'll report it. He's always been one to do things by the book.* A moment of silence filled the space. *But you're right.* The defeat in Jo's voice vanished. *We succeeded. Took a lot longer and cost a lot more, but we did it.*

And you'll do it again. Maxine felt a surge of pride, and it was well earned since she was now unofficially part of research and development.

Thanks for the encouragement. Jo's voice sounded better—hopeful and light. *Good night, hon. Sweet dreams. I love you.*

Love you too. A warmth spread throughout her body. She wished she could snuggle beside Jo and kiss her good night. *Sleep tight.*

After the robotic voice confirmed the transmission had ended, Maxine rolled onto her side, tucked her hands beneath the pillow, and closed her eyes. She listened to the quiet in the room, hoping she might hear her father speak again.

On Monday morning, Maxine heard the TV blaring from the living room. In response to more picketing, protests, and riots breaking out on Sunday regardless of the curfew, a statewide lockdown had been issued, according to the newscaster. Everyone was to stay inside their homes until further notice. Police were monitoring the neighborhoods. Anyone who violated the restrictions would be arrested and subject to jail time and a hefty fine.

Her mother slouched on the sofa with her head buried in her hands. "It's the end."

"No, Mom." Maxine gently squeezed her mother's shaking shoulder. She had not seen her mother cry in years. "It's just the government trying to get ahold of the situation."

She strode over to the window and drew the curtains aside. A patrol car was parked at the mouth of the cul-de-sac, preventing anyone from entering or leaving. She heaved a sigh. So much for Jo going to the office and working with Eli on the bug removal. Oh well. She shrugged. There was nothing she could do, especially since she had promised her father she would not worry.

"I'll go make breakfast."

"How can you eat during the end of the world?" Her mother lifted her head, her eyes red-rimmed and swollen, her face streaked with tears.

A softness filled her body, and she bent to kiss her mother's forehead. "Because I know Dad's watching over us. He won't let anything bad happen."

Her mother lurched back, and her gaze narrowed. "How do you know he's watching us?"

"He talked to me," Maxine said matter-of-factly.

"Since when?"

"Saturday." Maxine steeled her spine. "When you asked who I was talking to, I was talking with Dad."

Her mother gaped. "Not Joe?"

"Not Jo." Maxine strode out of the living room.

Her mother stood and followed her into the kitchen.

"Are you going crazy?"

Maxine grabbed two plates and set them on the counter. She unwrapped a loaf of bread and placed two slices into the toaster. "I'm part of a scientific study."

"When did this happen?"

"About a week ago." She buttered the first batch of toast and handed the plate to her mother. "I was only supposed to be able to communicate with certain people. But I started hearing the dead."

"Like your father?"

"And Patty." She buttered the second batch of toast and poured herself a mug of coffee. "Do you want some?" She waved the carafe.

"No, I'm fine." Her mother carried her plate back into the living room and perched on the sofa. "Why didn't you tell me this before?"

"It just started happening on Saturday." She sat on the chair next to the sofa and bit into the crispy toast before washing it down with a sip of bitter coffee. "There's a bug in the program. Once it's fixed, I won't be able to communicate with them anymore."

"What did your father say?" Her mother set the plate on the coffee table and clasped her hands in her lap and leaned forward.

Maxine didn't want to disappoint her, but she wasn't about to make up a conversation. "He told me not to worry."

"That's it?"

She nodded.

Her mother stared at her hands for a long moment, then grabbed the remote and turned off the TV. "I guess I don't need to keep watching this nonsense."

That night, after completing her studies, Maxine contacted Jo through the brain-to-brain software.

Any luck with Eli's team? She slipped underneath the covers and listened to the silence.

Her mother had gone to bed early, exhausted by the emotional overload of what had been happening. Even the stars outside seemed to ache.

Nothing can be done until the lockdown is over. Jo's voice sounded resolute. *Have you had any transmissions from heaven today?*

Maxine tucked her hands beneath her cheek. *No. But I told my mom about talking with my dad. She seemed to believe me.*

You told her about the brain-to-brain software?

She cringed at the sharpness of Jo's voice. Did the nondisclosure agreement extend to family?

I didn't mention the software. I said I was part of a study.

You aren't part *of the study. You're* outside *the study.*

Why did Jo have to be so technical about it?

Maxine grumbled. *I know, but she doesn't know.*

Why did you say anything? Jo raised her voice.

Maxine bit her lip and swallowed a whimper. She clutched her pillow tight against her chest to hold down the pain welling up from her solar plexus. *I thought she would find comfort in knowing my dad's okay in heaven.* She rolled over and closed her eyes, trying to find the peace she'd felt last night after talking with father. *Aren't you scared after everything that's happened?*

You mean, becoming a young woman?

That, and everything else. Maxine couldn't help but think of her mother glued to the TV, absorbing all the doom and gloom. *The protests, the riots, the lockdown, the randomness of waking up a different age in a different body.* She breathed through the tightness in her chest. *Aren't you afraid?*

A long silence filled the space in her mind.

Finally, Jo's voice returned. *Long before you were born, the world went through worse terrors. A disease threatened to wipe out civilization. We spent almost two years in and out of lockdowns. But we found a way through it. We'll find a way through these events too.* Jo sighed. *I'm sorry I yelled at you earlier. I just thought this software was between us. No one needs to know. Not even Eli. Promise me you won't tell anyone else.*

Who else would she tell? Her father? Patty? It wasn't like she was close with any of her classmates. But obviously, Jo needed the reassurance, so she offered it to her.

Sure. I promise.

CHAPTER 10

C lickety-clack, clickety-clack.

Maxine's fingers flew across the keyboard, typing up the remaining essay for her last final exam. She wrote about management styles—autocratic, democratic, bureaucratic, charismatic. Having never held a job, not even a summer job at a fast-food joint, Maxine's thoughts dwelled exclusively on theories, academic nonsense recited for an exam, to prove she had memorized what was needed, that she had been paying attention in class; it wasn't anything practical from experience, showing she could lead, could manage, could pioneer the next generation of employees into the brightly evolving world.

Maxine doubted she would be managing any corporation anytime soon. Sure, the protests and riots had ceased over the past three weeks once several school administrators struck deals with The Revolution to fund research to identify whatever was causing its young female population to disappear, being replaced with a startling number of elderly men. The concern for finding a cause and a cure extended beyond the university system. Congress—which had the exact opposite problem with its demographic suddenly shifting from men long past their prime to women barely old enough to vote —passed emergency legislation to fund research and provide mental health counseling to those individuals distressed about their bodies being usurped, their identities no longer under their control. The lockdown had ended shortly thereafter, although a ten o'clock curfew remained, possibly to discourage any other groups from demonstrating their frustrations.

Sonoma State University had refused to reopen its campus, although talks remained open for a possible in-person graduation the weekend before Memorial Day. Maxine wasn't holding her breath. She knew the odds weren't in her favor. With a good portion of her graduating class either too old to cross the stage or dead, she would most likely receive her diploma in the mail. Not that she cared either way. She only wanted to graduate, find a job, move out, and start a proper adult life with an apartment of her own.

Now she bobbed her head to the rhythmic beat of electronic music streaming through her headphones. The drone of the TV vibrated through the soles of her feet from the living room, where her mother watched the evening news. With a flourish, she typed the last word. She saved the document, then rested her eyes.

With a soft gaze, she stared at the far corner of the room. Faded sunlight filtered through the dangling strands of a broken cobweb near the window overlooking the backyard. A squiggly flash of light slithered across her vision.

How odd.

When it happened a third time, she felt a prickle of fear against her neck. Returning to the computer, she searched online for a possible explanation, finally landing on a popular medical website that labeled the repeated visual disturbance as *flashers and floaters*, a natural occurrence in aging eyes.

Aging eyes?

Blinking rapidly, she glanced away. A jolt of panic raced across her shoulders.

I'm too young for these symptoms.

After grabbing her phone off the desk, she sent a thought-to-text to Jo, who had uninstalled the brain-to-brain software after she told Eli she had received otherworldly transmissions. The phone felt cumbersome in her hands. Jo had tried to persuade her to sneak into the lab to have the software uninstalled, but Maxine had refused. She still held out hope she might hear from her father again.

—*Had a flash of light in my field of vision. Did you ever get these when you were older?*—

She stared at the screen, holding her breath, listening to the stutter in her chest.

—*No. But my ex-wife did when she went through perimenopause. Why? Are you getting them? Maybe you should see an ophthalmologist.*—

She released her breath, her hands shaking. The words appeared on the tiny screen as she thought.

—*Could I be switching, like Patty did?*—

—*IDK.*—

Jo didn't know. A flare of heat flashed through her body, and Maxine tossed the phone onto her bed and returned to her computer. She typed *symptoms of the switch for women becoming men*. A list of twenty indications filled the screen. She clicked and scrolled through each sign, weighing it against the inventory of how she felt. Sudden stiffness of the limbs, vision changes, hearing loss, balancing issues, high blood pressure, high cholesterol, diabetes, stroke ... each symptom getting worse, until it ended with death.

She shut down the computer and pushed back her chair and jogged down the stairs to the living room.

"All done with school?" her mother asked.

In the blue light from the TV, Maxine nodded and took a seat in the chair next to the sofa. She didn't want to alarm her mother or make her think that Maxine thought she was older than her mother was, but she needed to know.

"What does it feel like to get old?" she asked.

Her mother sat upright and muted the TV. Her gaze cut across and landed squarely on Maxine's face. "You switching?"

Maxine gulped and tucked her feet under her hips. "I don't know." She felt fine now, better than fine, as alert and flexible as she had before the odd flashes of light. "I'm scared."

"We're all scared," her mother said. "Nobody has any answers. Not even AI."

The walls seemed to close around them, and Maxine's throat was suddenly dry. But she did not move, did not get up to get a glass of water, did not flick her gaze from her mother's solemn face, did not shift her legs, even as they fell asleep beneath her weight. She wasn't much of a history student or a science student.

Was the switch something that had happened over the course of human evolution, or was this truly something new? Could someone with enough intelligence piece it together, like a cardboard puzzle with the colored pieces turned face down so all you could see was the gray backing?

So far, from what she had read and heard and witnessed, no one seemed capable of the task—or at least, no one had come forward, which made Maxine wonder if there was more money to be made from people switching than from them staying the same. Of course, whatever was most profitable made the best business sense.

That profitability in the matter made her feel worse, saddened and lonely and bereft without consolation, and she thought to her father, *I need you right now.*

The room was silent without the voices from the TV. Her mother, with a downturned mouth and glassy eyes, continued staring at Maxine.

Dad, are you there?

Maxine cut her gaze across to the TV. A meteorologist stood before a map, pointing to a swirl of white moving across the land like a ghost. She thought through the commands—*engage, transmit*—but nothing happened. Not even a buzz or hum or static.

The room ached with silence.

Dad?

Maxine bowed her head, wondering if the software had truly failed, like Jo had suggested, or if her father just didn't want to talk to her anymore.

"It's still early," Maxine said, parsing her words. "I'm wondering if I can see Jo. We haven't visited in person since lockdown began."

Her mother stared at her, and a furrow of wrinkles clouded her brow. "I'm not fond of you leaving, especially if you aren't feeling well. But I can't keep you inside forever."

Maxine stretched her legs. Pins and needles prickled the soles of her feet once she stood. "Thanks. I'll be back before curfew." She danced on the balls of her feet around the coffee table.

"Oh, Maxine," her mother called.

She paused beneath the threshold. The blood flowed through her veins, and the tingling sensation drained from her legs. "Yes?"

"Be careful out there." Her mother pursed her lips. "If either you or Joe shows any signs of switching, come home immediately. Understand?"

The awareness of her long-ago omission tugged at the edges of her mind, and she almost opened her mouth and told her mother the truth—*Jo switched; he's a young woman now; we could be twins*. Would the truth rip apart the peace they had enjoyed after she confided in hearing her father's voice from heaven?

Maxine didn't know, but she didn't want to risk losing the solidarity she felt with her mother. So, she nodded her understanding and kept her mouth shut, believing with the idealism of youth that some things were better left unspoken.

Maxine arrived at Jo's house ten minutes later. She stood on the porch, rang the doorbell, and waited. She had not seen Jo in person in almost a month, and the fuzzy video chats they'd had didn't account for the difference in size or the absence of touch.

"Hey, you," Jo said, stepping back and waving her inside. "Long time no see."

"I missed you." Maxine stepped into Jo's arms for a big hug, her head wedged between Jo's breasts. The softness surrounded her like a halo of pillows, and the intriguing scent of Jo's skin—a mix of lavender and flowers—comforted her.

"I can't believe the wicked witch let you leave home."

Maxine released Jo and examined her. She was dressed in casual clothes—an oversize T-shirt and sweatpants—but her face was full of makeup, and she still wore an ensemble of jewelry, like clip-on earrings, a gold braided necklace, and metal bracelets. She looked like she had come home from work and been too tired to remove the face paint and accessories.

Maxine strode over to the sofa and flopped on the soft cushions. "She's my well-intentioned mother, and the government is evil. I have to be home by ten and not midnight."

"True." Jo curled up next to her and grabbed her hand. "I can't believe it's you in the flesh." She squeezed her fingers. "I'm so thrilled. Tell me everything."

Maxine didn't know where to start. Sure, they sent messages every day and chatted several times during the week, but the conversations were always interrupted by work, school, or the demands of sleep. "I finished finals. The recruiters have stopped calling, so I guess I'm on my own to find a job."

"Don't worry. Once things get back to normal, I'm sure you'll find something."

"No word from the board?"

Jo flushed.

"You didn't ask for a policy exception?" Maxine withdrew her hand and tucked it in her lap. A fresh swipe of hurt rubbed against her. "I just want an entry-level position. I'm not asking to be the vice president."

"I'm sorry." Jo bowed her head, then rubbed her temples with her fingertips. "I've just been overwhelmed with the beta testing and now the FCC violation notice." She dropped her hands and heaved a sigh. "Eli reported the bug. I don't blame him. But it wouldn't have been such a big deal if the problem could be fixed."

"It can't?" Maxine bit her lower lip. "Does that mean anyone with the software can communicate with heaven?" She thought of all the possibilities—reunions with long-lost loved ones, proof of the afterlife, maybe even knowledge of the future.

"No, it's inconsistent. You and a handful of others experienced it. That's it." Jo twisted an earlobe, and a clip-on earring fell into her hand. She twirled the gem between her fingers. "It opens so many other concerns, especially privacy issues. The board has recommended shelving the project before the FCC suspends it."

"Can they do that?" Maxine shifted closer.

"The board has to vote, and the FCC has to investigate, but both can happen."

Maxine stared at Jo as if seeing her for the first time—a strange woman in an oversize T-shirt with mussed-up hair and sleepy eyes and stooped shoulders, not the confident man she knew and loved, dressed in a collared shirt and pressed slacks with perfectly groomed hair, alert eyes, and strong shoulders.

"Listen." Jo pocketed the clip-on earring and grabbed Maxine's hand and inched closer. "I'd really like it if you could stay the night. Not for sex. I'm on my period. But because I haven't seen you in a while and I need the emotional support."

The pleading in her eyes nagged at the edges of Maxine's consciousness. "You know I can't spend the night. My mother would kill me." She tried to squeeze reassurance into Jo's hand. She knew how tender and vulnerable she felt during her period, and she imagined Jo was feeling the same, possibly worse. "I promise to spend the night every now and then after I get a job and move out on my own. Okay?"

"No, it's not okay." Jo shook off her hand and stood. She paced back and forth across the floor, her hands clasped behind her back, just like the old Joe. "I offered to have you move in with me, and you declined. I won't tolerate this back-and-forth nonsense anymore. I've always loved you. But now I need you." She swiveled and pointed to the ground between them. "You need to decide if you're in or if you're out."

Was that a flare of anger flashing across Jo's eyes? Maxine felt her heart stutter, and her skin grew cold. The fire and determination of the man she loved blazed in this incandescent young woman. Frowning, Maxine swung her feet off the sofa and leaned forward. "What are you talking about?"

Jo flared her nostrils. "Move in, or we break up."

"What?" Maxine gulped at the ultimatum. All the spunk and verve she had withheld spewed forth. "I'm not your kid. You can't push me around. I'm your equal."

"Then prove it and move in with me."

"I can't." Maxine stood and grabbed her backpack. "I want to make it on my own." A spray of rainbow-colored light erupted in her field of vision, and she sank back down and palmed her hands over her eyes. "I need to see a doctor."

Jo rubbed her shoulder. "Is it your eyes again?"

She nodded.

"It's probably stress."

Maxine dropped her hands and lifted her chin. "My dad stopped talking to me."

"Maybe you should get the software uninstalled." Jo sat next to her. "It might be causing the vision changes."

An unsettling feeling rustled around her stomach, and she shook her head. "It's not the software." She met Jo's insistent gaze. Could she dare to move from one home into another without learning if she had what it took to make it on her own? She shivered, wondering if her options were already more limited than she imagined. "I think I might be switching."

"You don't know for sure," Jo said. "I didn't have any symptoms before I switched. Why should you?" She stroked her hair and kissed her forehead. "I don't want to lose you."

"And I don't want to be pressured to move in with you." She threaded her fingers through Jo's hand. "Don't you remember what it felt like when you needed to prove to the world you had what it took to be a success?"

Jo nodded. "But I'm not asking you to give up success. I'm asking you to live with me because I can't be a woman without you. I don't want to text you about what to wear or how to behave or ask why I'm feeling the way I'm feeling or what to do about it. I want you to be the first person I see when I wake up and the last person I touch before I go to sleep." She inhaled deeply and steadied her voice. "Maybe it's the damn hormones talking, but I don't want to live another day without you by my side."

She bent and kissed Maxine's lips. An unexpected jolt of pleasure rippled through Maxine's body, and she pulled away. Touching her scorched lips, she replayed the moist, pillowy sensation of the kiss repeatedly until her body flooded with lustful warmth.

"Are you okay?" Jo asked.

But Maxine heard, *Will you stay?*

As she recalled the government mandate, fear quivered in her legs. She glanced at the clock across the room. Nine thirty. She had a maximum of fifteen minutes before she had to leave. Unless she chose to stay. Forever.

"Are you okay?" Jo asked again.

"No, and neither are you," Maxine said. "No one is okay. The world isn't okay. Nothing is okay." She stood and gathered her backpack again. "I'm going home. If you want to break up with me, then do it. I won't be strong-armed into making a decision I'll regret." She strode across the room and turned the knob of the front door, and a brisk wind rushed into the room. "Good night."

"Wait." Jo raced over and placed her hands on Maxine's shoulders. "I'm sorry for pressuring you."

Maxine narrowed her gaze. She understood that Jo was hormonal. She would probably forget about this emotional outburst once her period ended and her hormones stabilized.

"Don't worry. I understand. Go take some Pamprin and get some sleep. You'll feel better tomorrow. Okay?"

"Will you go see an ophthalmologist?" Jo asked.

"I'll make an appointment tomorrow."

Maxine could read the disappointment in Jo's face when she gave her a quick kiss. She'd never seen that side of Joe when he was a man, and some part of her relished it.

In her car, before she started the engine, she glanced back at the house and waved to Jo, who stood by the window, watching her. A touching warmth spread throughout her body. It was good to be wanted, even if the desire was stronger than she preferred, and even better to be needed, even if it left her with no viable options.

She shifted into drive and pulled away from the curb. A sense of empowerment engulfed her. After a lifetime of obeying everyone else, she had taken charge and responded to Jo's ultimatum with one of her own. A thread had been tugged loose from within the tight confines of her life. She smiled, looking forward to how and what it would unravel, even if it meant being all alone.

"You're cutting it close, missy," Maxine's mom yelled from the living room.

Maxine cringed as soon as she stepped into the foyer. The time on her phone glowed nine fifty-five p.m. Did her mom ever sleep?

Dad, can you talk to her?

Silence rang back.

Maxine sagged her shoulders, missing that instant thought-to-thought communication. Why was the software not working any longer? Should she take Jo's advice and have it uninstalled?

"I don't like you hanging out with that old man. You deserve someone younger."

If only she knew …

Maxine steeled her back. "Take it easy. I'm home before curfew."

Before her mom could respond, she hoofed it up the stairs. In the bathroom, she brushed her teeth and washed her face. Her lips, swollen from kissing Jo, stung like they had been bitten by an insect. A bristle of annoyance shimmied up her spine, but she ignored it. She undressed and slipped beneath the covers in her bed, next to the window overlooking the backyard.

She thought of the closed-mouth kiss she had given Jo, nothing more than a full-fledged mouth-to-mouth peck, but an unsettling feeling lingered in her body. Try as she might, she could not fall asleep. She tossed and turned, tucking the sheets beneath her chin, until a heat wave caused her to toss off the covers for a few delicious moments before a breezy chill traveled up her legs, causing her to yank the sheets up to her shoulders again. Hot and cold. Cold and hot. What was wrong with her body? She didn't know herself anymore.

A montage of tonight's visit with Jo played in her mind, then stretched back further. She remembered connecting thought-to-thought with Jo throughout the day on little things that mystified her as a new woman— where to buy the best waterproof mascara, tricks on how to open tight jars, and reminders to shave her underarms and legs when wearing short sleeves and a skirt. Maxine had thought a sisterly feeling might develop toward Jo, but it never materialized. She still felt the same way about Jo regardless of whether she was a man or a woman.

Had she made the right decision to stay here with her mother? Would Jo honor that decision and not break up with her? Could she find a job that paid enough for her to afford an apartment? Or would she have to find a roommate? And how would Jo feel about her sharing space with another woman who wasn't her?

Closing her eyes, she pleaded with the only person she thought might understand her dilemma.

Patty, are you there?

Patty had chosen to live in the dorms her freshman year, then moved back home after a brief stint of living off campus with a handful of roommates. The noise and chaos didn't allow for much studying, and the hours she had to work to pay her share of expenses left her tired and moody. After she moved back home, she talked nonstop about the day she would move out again. For a while, Maxine and Patty had shared a dream of moving out together after graduation. Sadness descended upon her when she reflected on that failed dream. But she concentrated harder, trying to engage the software.

Patty, please, talk with me. I'm confused, and I need a friend.

She strained to listen. The dark enveloped her in silence. She raised her head, thinking she might have heard a sound, but it was only her mother's snores from downstairs.

CHAPTER 11

Maxine's decision to stand up to Jo worked in her favor. Jo didn't break up with her. The uneven power in their relationship shifted, with Maxine gaining respect and Jo losing dominance. Without the gender inequality tipping the scales one way or the other, an easy balance formed, giving both space and intimacy equal footing.

But this positive state of events didn't prevent Maxine from worrying, for the ophthalmologist confirmed her worst suspicions—she had eyes older than her chronological years. This news unsettled her. Between the joint aches in her hands, the vision problems, and an increasingly unsteady gait, she feared the worst—she was slowly transforming. Each morning, she repeated the same routine, touching her face for stubble (none), her breasts (still there), and between her legs (still empty). Only then would she leave bed and get on with her day.

Three weeks after she received her diploma by mail, Maxine found a job. She had wanted something in the telecommunications industry, but Jo could not get the board to pass a policy exception, and the university recruiter she had been working with kept forwarding leads she could not take without upsetting the delicate balance of her relationship with Jo. Even if she had not been dating Jo, she would have preferred to work for Jo and not one of her competitors.

So, she applied online for a delivery service. Not one of the nationwide chains, but a local company that sourced its employees with discrimination. She had to have a clear DMV record and pass a background check, a drug and alcohol test, and a timed shopping and delivery test. The whole process took two weeks, and at the end, when she was offered a part-time job for minimum wage, plus tips, she accepted.

Her first day was spent in training, shadowing another delivery driver. Her partner was a young man, freshly graduated from high school, who drove fast and braked quickly, like a jerky amusement park roller coaster. He double-parked, letting his car idle with Maxine in the passenger seat, while he strode up the sidewalk, rang a bell, and waited for someone to open the door.

"Your turn," he said at the next stop.

The heat had broken through the clouds, and Maxine felt a bit of perspiration along her neckline as she gathered up the bags from the trunk and hobbled up the walkway. With her elbow, she pressed the doorbell and waited, shifting the bags to adjust the weight.

"Hello." An old man pulled back the door. "Just set those on the floor. I've a bad back."

Maxine stepped inside and placed the bags on the kitchen table knowing the old man was too crippled to pick them up off the floor. The items had been purchased from a local grocery store, mostly produce and a few choice cuts of meat, enough to last a week.

"Thank you, ma'am," the old man said. "I've tipped you on the app."

Maxine glanced around the house and realized the old man had once been a young woman from the plush furnishings, the household plants, and the light and bright paintings on the candy-colored walls.

Back in the car, she fastened her seat belt.

"What took you so long?" her partner asked.

Maxine wanted to explain the situation—the old man with the bad back, the feminine touches in the living room, the fear of being seen in public, the gratitude for the in-home delivery service—but she couldn't find the words to capture what she was feeling, so she shrugged.

"You need to drop the bags on the doorstep and leave," he said, "or you won't make your numbers."

"Numbers?"

"Yeah, you have to make a minimum number of deliveries a day, or you're fired."

Maxine winced. Whatever happened to customer service?

"I don't know if I can do it," she said, grabbing the handle above her head while her partner made a sharp turn. "I care too much."

"Yeah, well, you should have thought about it before accepting the job."

"I didn't think a small company would have so many demands."

"It's business. We're competing with the bigger name brands. We have to be faster, cheaper, better."

Faster, cheaper, better. Not exactly what she'd studied in business management courses, but the theory was sound and relatable. The most profitable company always won. Who cared what it took to get there, right?

But Maxine needed a job. Any job. To save enough money to move out on her own, without Jo's help. She tightened her grip on the handle as traffic slowed and her partner slammed on the brakes. She jerked back and forth, feeling like her body might snap in half.

"Okay. I promise to do better at the next stop. Just don't drive so recklessly. I'd like to make it home in one piece."

The sky was covered in a misty fog when Maxine woke on her first solo day at work. After a reassuring shower, in which she touched her cheeks (no stubble), breasts (no muscle), and between her legs (no testicles), she dressed and came downstairs for breakfast. She found her mother hunched over a bowl of cold cereal, the printed newspaper spread out beside her on the table, tsk-tsking as she read.

"Look here," she said, jabbing the newsprint. "Somebody killed themselves over switching."

Maxine peered over her mother's shoulder. The local press had dedicated a three-inch column to the event, in which an old man, now a young woman, had hung themselves from the rafters in the garage. Their eighty-year-old wife commented that she had found the body dangling like a piñata and called the police, assuming a suicide, although no note was found. The article cited a well-respected psychologist from Stanford, who stated depression was a common symptom of the switch, and anyone experiencing the switch should consult with their medical provider for assistance to avoid such an unnecessary ending. Help was possible.

"Just you wait and see," her mother said, wagging a finger. "The end of the world is near."

Maxine didn't believe in the doomsday prophecies her

mother made, but she knew the threat of switching was real. She had witnessed Patty's and Joe's transformations. Why not her next? Or her mother? Or the neighbors? Or anyone?

Not wanting to read about any more catastrophes, Maxine padded into the kitchen to make cinnamon toast and coffee.

Her mother kept reading the paper. Every now and then, she huffed or shook her head. The paper rattled in her hands when she turned and folded the pages. She was the only one Maxine knew who still subscribed to a physical newspaper. Everyone else she knew read the news online.

"More coffee, Mom?"

"No, dear."

After pouring herself a cup, she sat beside her mother. She crunched the crisp edges of the sugary-sweet toast between her teeth, chewing slowly, knowing she wouldn't have to worry about making deliveries in bumper-to-bumper traffic since her shift started after the morning commute ended.

"Look here," her mother said, poking at another story. "Your boyfriend made the business section."

He did?

She hadn't spoken with Jo since the FCC had suspended the brain-to-brain project after completing their investigation. An emergency board meeting was called, and Jo was so upset that she didn't want to talk about it. Whatever had transpired during that meeting was so devastating that Jo didn't want Maxine to visit, so Maxine had left her alone.

A curious tension tightened across Maxine's jaw, and she stopped chewing. Had Jo gone to bed a woman and woken up a man again? She took a sip of the bitter coffee to wash down the dry toast before wiping her hands on a napkin and grabbing the paper from her mother's hands.

"Hey, I was reading that, missy."

Maxine ignored her mother's comment. She scanned the stories before landing on the headline, "FCC Suspends B2B Project After CEO Switches." Five inches of print were dedicated to this story, even though it was buried on the second page of the Business section. Maxine skimmed over the text, searching for meaning beyond the headline, but the story just droned on and on about how the sixty-year-old Joseph had transformed into a twenty-something young woman who had recently changed her name to Josephine. Finally, in the last two paragraphs, the story mentioned the FCC investigation and suspension of the brain-to-brain software after a bug caused a breach between the human and divine worlds, which allowed for users to experience extrasensory perception. As a result, the board of directors had voted to place Joe/Jo on probation for the regulatory violation until further notice.

Maxine's mouth went dry. No wonder Jo hadn't wanted to talk yesterday. The software project had been canceled, and Jo's future at the company she'd founded was precarious. At the bottom of the article, Maxine noticed the side-by-side color photographs, documenting the before and after of Jo's spontaneous transition. A cold sweat broke out along Maxine's hairline. Her secret, the one she should have told her mother, was splashed across the news.

Her mother, who had been reading over her shoulder, yanked the paper away and jabbed at the photos. "Are you a lesbian now?"

Heat rushed to Maxine's face. "No." The word spewed from her mouth, horrible and reflexive, making her worry she was, indeed, a lesbian.

She closed her eyes for a moment, imagining the news rippling through her extended family like a stone cast into a pond. When she opened her eyes, she found her mother glaring.

"How long have you known?"

"Known what?" Maxine tried to be cagey. She wanted to bide her time, see if she could scramble with a solution to her mother's indignation.

"About his switching?" Her mother rattled the newspaper in her hands. "The article says the company has been going downhill since he became a woman. I'm asking you how long you've kept this a secret from me."

Maxine gulped. She scraped her chair back and stood, grabbing her plate. "Not that long."

"You lied to me." Her mother threw down the paper and stood, blocking an exit from the dining room. "You told me you heard your father speak. And I believed you."

"I *did* hear him speak."

"It wasn't him. It was a software bug."

"It was him." Maxine slammed the plate on the dining room table. "Didn't you read the article? Or did you just look at the pictures?"

Her mother gasped. "I can read."

"Then you would know the difference between the software bug *creating* Dad's voice and the software bug *allowing me to hear* Dad's *actual* voice."

Her mother crossed her arms over her chest. "You still lied about your boyfriend."

Maxine sighed. She had no defense against that statement.

"As long as you live under my roof, you may not see him anymore," her mother said.

Bowing her head, Maxine flared her nostrils. She wished the software still worked so she could contact her father. He could talk sense into anyone, and she was certain he would explain things to her mother. Love had no boundaries, knew no distinction between man and woman, but only existed as a matter of choice, and that choice should not be criticized or condemned, and the chooser should never be shamed into feeling guilty.

"Did you hear me?"

Her mother's shrill voice chilled Maxine to the core. She shuddered.

"Yes, I heard you." She lifted her head and narrowed her gaze at her mother. If she could dart lasers from her pupils, she would have. "No more seeing Jo as long as I live here."

"I never liked him as an old man. I hate him more as a young woman."

Maxine shoved her shoulders back, her body trembling with emotion. "Like you hate me?" She tapped a fist between her breasts, the edges of her voice straining.

Her mother's mouth gaped, but she said nothing.

"I have to go to work," Maxine said.

She knew her mother had an app on her phone that could pinpoint her location, but she didn't know if her mother knew how to use it. Either way, she planned on uninstalling the software once she entered her car. She needed to visit Jo after her shift ended. To talk about the article. To talk about her mother. To talk about the future. She would stay away as long as she could without breaking curfew.

As soon as her mother moved away from the doorway, Maxine bounded up the stairs.

"Don't think you can fool me." Her mother's voice slapped against her back. "If you're not home by the time your shift ends, I'll know where you are, and I will lock you out of the house. You will never live with me again."

Pausing on a step, Maxine counted her breaths. *One, two, three …*

"Don't threaten me."

"I'm serious," her mother said.

A flash of several potential futures panned before Maxine. She could accept Jo's proposal to move in together. She imagined positioning her dresser in Jo's bedroom, setting up her laptop on the kitchen table, storing her clothes in a shared closet. The mathematical part of her brain tabulated the cost. Would Jo ask her to pay rent? Probably not. But she couldn't assume. Jo was a businessperson, like herself, and treated relationships accordingly. The other part of her brain calculated the expense of staying. Her mother was an emotional vampire, sucking all the lifeblood from her with doom and gloom and conspiracy theories, leaving her with little energy. But could she tough it out for a few more weeks until she saved enough for a deposit on an apartment? Her stomach churned, and acid filled the back of her throat.

"Did you hear me?" her mother repeated. "I'm serious."

Still thinking of her options, she turned to face her mother. "I'm serious too." She gripped the banister and took a step downward. "Don't threaten me."

"What you going to do about it?" Her mother punched her waist with her fists and broadened her stance like a bully on the playground.

Maxine examined the defiant tilt of her mother's chin. She didn't need to play this tug-of-war for power. She could bow out, leave, forget this conversation had happened. Turning, she let the silence speak for her.

CHAPTER 12

Maxine pulled into the twelve-acre business park that housed Jo's office to deliver lunch to several employees. She strode into the lobby of the main campus. Her sneakers squeaked on the polished marble floor. She stopped to speak with the receptionist behind a glass partition.

"Deliveries for the data center," she said after consulting her notes.

The receptionist took the bags that smelled of barbeque chicken and pulled pork from the eatery downtown.

Although Maxine had only been on the job for two hours, she decided to take her ten-minute break. "Is Jo Capaldi available? I'm Maxine, her girlfriend."

The receptionist, who sat beside a name plate that read *Daisy*, picked up the phone and dialed. Her solemn gaze flicked across Maxine's face. "Heather, I have a Maxine for Jo. Should I detain her or send her up?" She listened, nodded briefly, then hung up the receiver. "I need to scan your ID. You'll need to sign in and wear this." She slid a visitor badge across the counter.

Maxine complied with the requests. Afterward, she rode the elevator to the top floor. She had only visited Joe once, when he needed a ride to and from work while his car was being serviced, but she only pulled up to the circular drive and dropped him off at the front doors. She had never been inside this palatial space with its tall ceilings and echoey halls and plush elevators lined with wood paneling and mirrors.

When the elevator stopped and the doors slid open, Maxine stepped into a wide hallway. Daisy had said to turn right and head straight back, so that was what Maxine did. She passed by several offices with glass windows and closed doors, where people sat, hunched over computers. At the end of the hallway, the space opened into a broad reception area with white sofas and sleek coffee tables and abstract artwork in neutral colors.

"Heather, it's Maxine." She recognized the executive assistant from Jo's description—middle-aged brunette with a boxy blazer and photos of her ten-year-old son positioned proudly on her desk.

"Is Jo expecting you?" Heather slipped on a pair of reading glasses and consulted the calendar on her computer monitor. She frowned. "I don't have you penciled in."

"It's an emergency." Maxine bit her lower lip and clasped her hands, hoping Jo wasn't out for lunch or in a meeting. She had failed to send a thought-to-text, as she had only planned on making the delivery.

"She's not at her desk," she said, "but I'll page her." Heather picked up the receiver, pressed a button, and spoke. "Jo Capaldi, please return to your desk. Maxine is waiting."

The voice carried over the loudspeaker, filling the entire building with Heather's sweet voice.

"Have a seat." Heather smiled and waved toward the sofas.

Maxine perched on the edge of the nearest sofa. She fumbled with her phone, checking the time. Only five minutes left. She tapped her foot against the thick carpeting and shoved her phone back into a pocket.

"Maxine." Jo rounded the corner. "What brings you here?"

Jo wasn't alone. An attractive man in his late twenties, dressed in a sharp suit, stood beside her. He looked familiar with large brown eyes and soft brown curls, but she couldn't place him until he spoke.

"Hi, Maxi. Did you come to take Jo to lunch?"

She gasped. Eli. She didn't recognize him without the scraggly beard, plaid shirts, and khaki slacks. He had also lost weight—about twenty pounds, she guessed—and the difference was striking. Why hadn't Jo said something?

"Actually, no," Maxine said, though a lunch break sounded better than the couple of minutes she had left. "I need to talk to her. It's an emergency."

"Is your mom all right?" Jo asked, taking her by the elbow and steering her toward the office. She paused, glancing over her shoulder. "I'll come see you after I'm done." Her voice was soft, almost sensual.

Eli nodded. Maxine watched how his gaze slithered up and down the length of Jo's body, taking in the fullness of her breasts, the curve of her waist, and the length of her legs in those to-die-for heels. A twinge of jealousy tightened across her chest. Why hadn't Jo mentioned Eli's crush on her?

Jo swiped a key card from a lanyard around her neck, and the door unlocked. "Have a seat." She ushered Maxine inside the cool cavern with its blond furniture and floor-to-ceiling windows, overlooking the greens of the campus gardens.

Maxine spun around to face Jo. "My mom read the article about you in today's paper. She's forbidden me to see you as long as I live under her roof."

"That's the emergency?" Jo asked, striding around the massive desk. She plunged into a chair that looked like a white cloud and rocked back, crossing her legs. "I thought she was sick or had switched or something. Why didn't you just send a thought-to-text?"

"Because I was here, making deliveries." Maxine fluttered her hands. She gulped a mouthful of air and steadied her voice. "I can't come to your house tonight. Or any other night."

"You're making this much more complicated than it is." Jo steepled her fingers and trained her gaze.

The silence broke through the hysteria that had been building inside Maxine. Something deflated inside of her, and she felt infantile in her impulsivity to come here to complain. Of course, it was no big deal for Jo. Jo wanted her to move in with her. Her mother's ultimatum forced Maxine's hand. Move in or break up. The unfairness suddenly seemed both inconsequential to Jo and monumental to Maxine. For the first time, Maxine felt the starkness of their age gap—not in terms of physical years, which had narrowed to the point of being nonexistent, but in terms of wisdom gained from living, for which there was no solution. Jo housed a wealth of experience Maxine lacked. Nothing would change that fact.

She gulped. "I'm sorry for bothering you. I'll go."

"That's it?" Jo stood and stalked around the desk. "Not even a hug or kiss goodbye?"

Maxine pouted. She felt five years old again, standing on the sidewalk, waiting for the bus to come pick her up, her parents demanding a last-minute hug or kiss goodbye. But Jo wasn't her parent. She was her girlfriend. No, she was only an older adult, someone who Maxine had mistaken for a lover when what she needed was a mentor to shepherd her into a career. Jo had never intended to be that guide. That was why Maxine was stuck making deliveries instead of answering phones here. After a whole year, she finally, finally, finally understood the situation. Too bad she was too late to benefit from the knowledge.

With her fingertips, Jo tipped Maxine's chin and planted a kiss on her brooding lips. "Don't be so glum. You're saving to move out, right? So, what's not seeing each other for a few weeks? We've survived not seeing each other during lockdown. We can survive this." Jo pulled her into a hug.

Maxine breathed the sweet floral scent of Jo's perfume. She didn't need to consult her phone to know more than ten minutes had passed. "I have to get back to work."

"Video chat tonight?" Jo held open the door.

Nodding, Maxine slipped out of the office and strode down the hallway to the elevator, feeling the strangeness of something infinitesimally small shift at the center of her being. She could not name it if asked, but it was there —a tiny, blinking reminder that she was no longer the same person she had been when she walked in through the lobby doors.

"Where you going?" Her mother sat on the sofa, craning her neck.

Maxine stood in the doorway with a box propped

against one hip. It was full of knickknacks from the top of her dresser—photos of her family in happier times, perfume bottles from Jo, and figurines her father had bought her, one for each birthday, each time saying they would be valuable someday.

"I'm moving," she told her mother.

"Already?"

Maxine nodded, then disappeared out the front door. The sun had set, and a brisk chill accompanied the haunting twilight. It was the week before the Fourth of July, and American flags were flapping from the front porches of her neighbors' homes. A sense of freedom filled her lungs. She popped open the trunk of her sedan and placed the box inside, then returned upstairs to her bedroom to carry down her clothes, books, laptop, and toiletries. When she was finished, she stood for a long moment in the center of the room, wondering if she should come back on the weekend to get the heavier items or if she should leave all the furniture in the event her mother wanted to rent out her room.

"Where you living?" her mother asked.

Maxine gasped, spinning around to face her mother, who stood in the doorway. "Around." She did not want to give her mother the address.

"Is this because of what I said this morning?" Her mother tilted her head to one side, her eyes filling with moisture.

"I've been wanting to leave since I graduated. Aren't you happy for me?"

Her mother heaved a sigh. "I'd be happier if I knew where you were living."

"No, you wouldn't." Maxine shouldered past her mother and bounded down the stairs.

"You going to live with that lesbian, aren't you?" Her mother's voice trailed ahead of her feet, slamming into Maxine's back.

Maxine kept striding across the living room to the front door. "I don't have to take this abuse anymore."

"Fine," her mother said. "Be that way."

Maxine slammed the front door and hopped into the front seat of her car. She started the engine and pulled away from her childhood home, which housed most of her memories. Swallowing her frustration, she snapped on the radio and listened to a top 40 song. The same droning lyrics about grief and loss and love filled the space around her.

When she parked outside Jo's house, she sat in the car for a moment longer. Jo's sports car was probably parked in the garage since the lights were burning through the curtains in the window. She had not told Jo she was coming, had not sent a thought-to-text or left a voice mail message, had just assumed the offer still stood.

Taking a deep breath, she opened the door and strode up the walkway. She rang the bell and waited.

Jo yanked the door back and raised her eyebrows. "I thought we were video chatting tonight."

Maxine gulped. "I thought I'd take you up on your offer and move in with you."

"Tonight?"

Maxine turned around and popped open the trunk of her sedan. "I brought all my stuff."

"Oh, baby." Jo grabbed her hand and pulled her into the house and held her for a long moment. "Are you sure? I thought you wanted to live on your own first."

"I did," Maxine said, her voice muffled against Jo's shoulder. "But what you said to me today changed my mind."

"What did I say?" Jo took a step back and held Maxine by the shoulders.

The concern and tenderness in Jo's voice was a stark contrast to her mother's venom and accusations.

"You said I was making things more complicated." She cupped her hands against Jo's waist. "You were right. I don't have to live on my own to prove my independence. I can be me with you. Separate and together. What do you say?"

"I say you're wise beyond your years." Jo smiled and dropped her hands to the sides. "Now let's go get your things."

CHAPTER 13

Maxine blinked awake in a nest of tangled sheets. The gray light of early morning filtered through the plantation shutters and cast a pall of doubt on her condition. Her heartbeat stuttered in her chest. She touched her face (smooth), patted her breasts (still there), and reached between her legs (empty). She exhaled and waited for her heart rate to slow to a pitter-patter.

"Morning," Jo said.

The scent of freshly roasted coffee wafted into the room. Jo set a mug on the nightstand and rejoined her in bed.

The stark glow of the clock on the nightstand read six fifteen. Maxine snuggled against the pillows and grabbed the warm mug. It was a workday, but she didn't have to leave for another three hours. The prospect of time stretched like an open highway.

She took a sip of the rich brew, sweetened with whole milk and raw sugar. "Mmm. This is good."

"It should be. It costs more than they charge at those chain stores." Jo tipped her head back and sighed. The steam from the mug curled around her face. "It's good to have money."

Maxine never asked how much money Jo had. She felt

the question was more of an intrusion than a curiosity.

"Would you like scrambled eggs or French toast for breakfast?" Jo asked.

A choice. How rare. She was used to making her own meals at her mother's house. Would Jo be cooking every day for her?

"French toast, please." She took another sip of hot coffee and stretched out her legs, her big toe brushing up against Jo's calf.

Memories of last night floated all around her like bubbles. Sunlight streamed through the plantation shutters and cast pale stripes across the soft bedding. The moment felt as surreal as the last handful of weeks had been.

Jo reached across Maxine's lap for the remote on the nightstand. She turned on the TV against the opposite wall.

Three medical specialists huddled in a circle on *Good Morning America*. When they spoke, their names appeared on a banner beneath them. A dark-skinned man, dressed in a blue pin-striped suit, crossed a leg over a knee and leaned forward to kick off the debate. The banner said he was Dr. Roberto Hernandez, an endocrinologist. Dr. Hernandez claimed the proliferation of men becoming women and women becoming men was caused by a radical shift in hormone production.

"But it only affects a certain segment of the population," he said, "specifically men over the age of fifty-five and women between the ages of eighteen and forty."

Eighteen to forty. That's me. Maxine sputtered, and a drizzle of coffee splattered against her nightshirt.

"Are you okay?" Jo asked.

"Yeah, I'm fine." She wiped the coffee from her mouth with the back of her hand and listened to the experts.

"That doesn't explain the rapid aging in both directions," said Dr. Zoe Chen, a geriatrician. She was a petite woman who wore her black hair in a severe bob. The boxy white pantsuit was a stark contrast to her black stiletto heels. "Hormones aren't solely responsible. I think something larger is at play."

"Maybe a mutation," Dr. Roy Levin, a medical geneticist, said. He was an older man with fuzzy gray eyebrows that wiggled like caterpillars when he spoke. "My team is currently testing affected people. My guess is, the problem exists either at the DNA or chromosomal level. The transformation is possibly triggered by environmental factors, like air or water."

"Water, exactly," Dr. Chen said. "The body needs adequate hydration to avoid the ravages of aging." She crossed her ankles and tucked them close against the pedestal chair. Her hands fluttered like butterfly wings when she spoke. "People aren't drinking water anymore. Everyone opts for designer coffees and cocktails, all of which adds to dehydration."

"This problem is not caused by dehydration," Dr. Hernandez said. "It's directly related to hormonal changes."

"From a possible rearrangement of genes or chromosomes," Dr. Levin said.

Maxine set the mug on the nightstand, grabbed the remote, and switched off the TV. "I can't watch this stuff. It's all my mother listened to when I lived with her."

"I'm sorry." Jo patted Maxine's hand before confiscating the remote. She turned the TV back on and switched to the weather channel. A meteorologist pointed to a map and rattled off the projected temperatures for today. Jo lowered the volume and set aside the remote. "I like to listen to something while I get ready for work. It makes me feel like I'm not alone."

"You're not alone anymore." Maxine leaned over Jo's lap and seized the remote. She turned off the TV. "I'm here. I'll talk to you as you get ready."

Jo stared at the remote. "You're not upset about what I watch. You're upset about what that doctor said about women between the ages of eighteen and forty being affected."

"Wouldn't you be?" Maxine gripped the remote tighter and crossed her arms over her chest. "Don't you miss being a man?"

"No, I don't," Jo said. "I like being a woman."

"You do?" Maxine gaped.

The confession seemed odd. No one she knew said they liked the fact that they had switched into the opposite gender. Everyone she knew wanted their bodies back.

"The world is quieter and more peaceful," Jo said, staring off into the distance. "I used to be so outwardly focused, but the hormones make me aware of my body in ways I took for granted." She inhaled deeply, took a sip of coffee, and sighed. "It's like taking off my shoes to walk barefoot on the dirt. I'm centered and rooted, here in my body, and the rest of the world orbits out there, but I'm no longer spinning endlessly with it. I'm here, in my body, rooted where it matters." She frowned, facing Maxine. "Does that make sense?"

It didn't. Not to Maxine. She had never felt so mystically connected to her female body. Her cycles, though regular from the pill, didn't control her the way they did Jo. "No, it doesn't. I think it's easier being a man. You get instant respect."

Jo laughed. "I do miss the hearty handshakes and the insider status of the good ol' boys' club."

"Exactly," Maxine said. "But I don't think I want to become a man. Especially not an old man."

"No one wants to be old," Jo said. "We live in a culture constantly seeking the fountain of youth." She finished her coffee and slipped out of bed. "I'll go make breakfast. I promise no TV if you come in the kitchen to keep me company, okay?"

Maxine unfolded her arms and set the remote on the nightstand. She grabbed her mug of coffee and padded after Jo. Her bare feet slapped against the cool hardwood floor. With her fingertips, she rubbed the side of the warm mug. She hoped Dr. Hernandez was mistaken and the phenomenon didn't affect every woman between the ages of eighteen and forty, only some of them.

CHAPTER 14

Living with Jo was much easier than living with her mother. Maxine didn't have a curfew. Jo didn't care how late she stayed out as long as she knew where she was.

"For emergencies," she said.

Maxine didn't have to listen to doom-and-gloom TV. Jo just needed background noise, and Maxine was happy to supply it, peppering her with details from her day. But the best part was knowing Jo was the first person she saw each morning and the last person she saw each night.

Tonight, a month after she had moved into Jo's house, Maxine sat at the dining table, eating the Mediterranean salad Jo had prepared for dinner. She didn't cook every night. Some days, they had takeout, but on those nights she did cook, the food was almost always something Maxine would have never eaten with her mother.

Jo had just finished talking about the changes she wanted to make at work now that the brain-to-brain project had been permanently suspended. She wanted to boost company morale, not to mention the stock prices, after everything had plummeted.

"You want to what?" Maxine almost dropped her fork against the bowl. She wasn't sure she had heard Jo correctly, and she wanted to give her the benefit of the doubt.

"Start the day with yoga and meditation." Jo spread a slice of tomato with hummus. "You're always telling me to be more mindful."

"At home, not at work," Maxine said.

Jo had a habit of going about the day, forgetting Maxine was near, and often ran into her in the hallway or knocked against her in the kitchen. The shock of remembering she was no longer living alone startled her, and she would gasp and sputter a slew of apologies before laughing about her absentmindedness.

Jo finished eating the hummus and tomato and took a sip of water. "I want to set the mood or the tone for the day." She waved her hands, trying to mimic what she wanted to create in the workplace, something fluid and airy. "And nothing works better than movement and breathing."

Maxine screwed her lips like she had bitten into something rotten and disgusting. "The board will never approve."

"I don't need board approval. Chris said so himself." A smug smile graced Jo's face.

With a downcast gaze, Maxine dragged her fork through the kale in her salad. "Eli will find a way to sabotage your efforts."

She blamed Eli for everything wrong with Jo's company—from his reporting the breach between human and divine communications to the uneasy feeling of encroachment she felt whenever Jo mentioned him. He was not to be trusted, but Jo had dismissed her concerns, calling her "a paranoid girlfriend." Jo had said she wasn't interested in men despite the urge she felt to procreate each month during ovulation. She swore she battled against the hormones with all her reasoning, and so far, she had avoided unnecessary flirtation. She even bought a fake engagement ring she wore to fend off strangers who would otherwise ask her out on a date. Maxine thought her efforts were sincere but misguided. No man willing to bed a beautiful woman cared whether she was married, and no amount of logic could eliminate the biological clock ticking in Jo's womb. Loyalty, Maxine knew, was beyond hormones or reasoning. It was a personality trait ingrained through habit and love, both of which Maxine feared Jo didn't have enough of to prevent an eventual disaster.

"Why such a Debbie Downer?" Jo stared at Maxine.

The uncomfortable gaze triggered an irritable undercurrent in the power grid of Maxine's calm exterior. True, she was depressed. She blamed it as part of the biological structure she had inherited from her mother.

She set her fork aside and folded her hands in her lap. With a steady voice, she announced, "I'm late for my period, and I'm not pregnant."

"So?" Jo shrugged. The divot between her eyebrows narrowed into a slit of concern.

"So, something's wrong with my body." Maxine released her hands and grabbed the cloth napkin from the table. During a recent shopping spree, Jo had purchased linens for the table because paper napkins were "uncouth." But Maxine missed shredding the paper between her fingers to ease her anxiety. "I called to schedule an appointment with my OB-GYN, but the next available spot isn't until next month." She flipped the napkin over and over in her lap. "The wait wouldn't normally be a problem, but my mom texted to let me know she's cutting me off from insurance at the end of this month." She took a breath and lifted her gaze. "I have to wait another thirty days to get insurance at my job, which is fine—I can wait—but I'm scared something's wrong with my body right now."

"Don't worry." Jo stretched her arm across the table and patted the back of Maxine's hand. "We'll figure it out."

"How?" Maxine jerked her hand free.

Her father had told her not to worry, and when he was talking with her on a regular basis, Maxine had not worried. But he was gone, as was Patty, and the software she had installed just idled in her brain like a useless junkyard car. She should have it uninstalled, like Jo had suggested, but moments like this—when worry pulsed through her body and messed with her mind—left her hoping against reason that her father's voice might cut through the craziness and tell her everything was going to be all right.

Jo rapped her fingernails on the table. She had started getting weekly manicures—a luxury Maxine envied, but could not afford—and the glossy shine further infuriated Maxine, who could not understand how her boyfriend-turned-girlfriend was more stylish and beautiful than she was.

"Let's get married," Jo said. "That way, I can add you to my insurance immediately."

Maxine shook her head. "No way. I don't want to get married just to get insurance."

"But I love you. We'd be marrying for love."

"You said you never wanted to get remarried after your divorce. Why did you change your mind?"

Jo curled her hands into fists. "I'm a woman now. I feel differently about a lot of things. Marriage included."

She knocked her knuckles against the table. "I also want children someday."

"Children?" Maxine gasped. She didn't know Jo anymore. The man she had fallen in love with only wanted a young plaything on his arm. This man-turned-woman wanted the American dream of a spouse and a family. "Next, you'll say you want a dog."

"Dogs are too much responsibility. You have to walk them every day."

"And a baby isn't?" Maxine guessed Jo had never babysat. "They require constant care. Feeding, burping, changing, bathing. It never ends."

"Okay, we're getting off topic." Jo raised the glass of water to her lips. "You're probably just worrying about nothing. I'm late for my period when I'm stressed."

"I'm on the pill. I'm never late."

"But you are stressed. I've noticed I'm late whenever I'm under pressure."

Maxine bowed her head. Yes, she was stressed. About her body.

The silence stretched like taffy—long, sticky, and never-ending.

Maxine never thought they would be that couple who had to steer the conversation back to safe topics. But they were.

"So," she said, retrieving her fork and stabbing it into her salad, "when will daily yoga and meditation start?"

"Next week." Jo smiled, and the conversation ended.

For now.

CHAPTER 15

That night, in bed, Maxine rolled away from Jo's touch. She tugged the sheets up to her chin and tucked her hands beneath her cheek and closed her eyes to go to sleep. In the morning, she didn't respond to Jo's questions about breakfast or her schedule for the day. She even dodged Jo's kiss goodbye.

On the second day, Jo complained. "I don't know you anymore. You used to be so chatty, but now you hardly talk."

"I'm leaving for work." Maxine grabbed her backpack.

She used work as an excuse to get out of the house, even when she didn't have deliveries until hours later. She would find a café, where she could read a book, or visit a park and sit beneath the shade of a tree, or walk the foothills surrounding the city. Anything to avoid being near Jo or being in Jo's house.

The avoidance tactics weren't something Maxine was proud of doing, but a necessary evil. She needed to preserve her sanity, carve out a space just for herself, be alone. At least, when she had lived with her mother, she'd had her own room. She could close the door and pretend she was somewhere else. With Jo, she had nowhere to go. The open-floor plan left her no room in which to hide. And as the days progressed, she felt more and more like hiding.

One afternoon, sitting on a bench at a neighborhood park, she sent a text to her mother.

—*I'm sorry. Please forgive me. I want to come home.*—

She cradled the phone in her hands, staring at the thought bubbles on the screen, wondering what her mother was typing.

—*You made your bed. Now go lie in it.*—

Maxine gasped. She glanced up. A couple of rollerbladers skated by, and a handful of pigeons settled near her feet. They stretched their necks and pecked at the ground, searching for remnants of other people's meals. The phone felt warm in her hands. She turned it over and thought maybe she had misunderstood her mother. So, she tried again.

—*If I break up with Jo, may I move back home?*—

—*No.*—

—*Why not?*—

—*You smart. Figure it out.*—

Maxine cupped the phone in her hands. The sunlight dappled her skin and cast long shadows near the bench where she sat. She inhaled sharply and steadied the thoughts flying through her mind about how much she hated her mother, how much she wanted Jo to understand her worries, how much she missed hearing from her father, and how much she needed to see a doctor to confirm she was still a healthy young woman.

—*If I come home, I promise to obey you.*—

—*So what?*—

—*I'll cook and clean and make your life easier.*—

—*Ha! My life is easier. I can turn up the TV as loud as I want. I can eat whatever I want. And I don't have to worry about an ungrateful child missing curfew. My life is good.*—

The vitriol left a sour taste in Maxine's mouth. She had never meant to hurt her mother.

—*I'm not ungrateful.*—

—*Does your girlfriend keep you on a tighter leash? That why you want to come back?*—

—*She doesn't give me a curfew.*—

Maxine leaned against the rough bench, thinking of her situation. Jo didn't dominate her. She didn't harass her. She didn't do any of the things her mother had done to annoy her. She just wanted to get married and have a family. Why couldn't Maxine accept that change of opinion without freaking out so badly that she wanted to move back in with her crazy mother?

—*I'm sorry, Mom. Isn't that enough?*—

—*You should have listened to me. Now you're stuck figuring things out on your own.*—

A burning sensation ignited in Maxine's chest. She wanted to tell off her mother, but that would only prove she was an immature person who had not learned any lessons from moving away from home. So, she signed off.

—*OK. Thanks. Talk with you again soon.*—

Before she could tuck her phone into her backpack, she heard it ping one more time. She swiped the screen and read her mother's message.

—*Don't bother.*—

A cold sensation shimmied up her back. She was officially estranged from her mother. How had that happened? She bit her lower lip, shoved the phone into her backpack, and stood to leave. She was a few hundred dollars short of having the first, last, and security deposit for a studio apartment, and her employer would not advance her the funds in the event she quit before being repaid. So, she would have to tough things out. Reconcile with Jo. Figure out a way to win at this thing called life.

That night, Maxine came home immediately after her shift ended. Jo wordlessly set the dining room table and served up leftovers.

Maxine sat beside her, cutting her chicken into tiny squares, fluffing the rice with the tines of her fork, and shoveling her vegetables from one side of the plate to another like a child playing with her food.

"Are you going to tell me what's wrong?" Jo tapped her fork against her plate, the tinny sound reverberating like mini shock waves through the otherwise silent room.

Maxine widened her eyes and flared her nostrils like a bull that had been roused to fight. She had noticed subtle changes in her body over the past week, nothing alarming. Just some aches and pains. A lot more strands in her hairbrush. Once, under the glare of the bathroom lights, she'd spotted some gray roots.

"I don't feel like myself, and I don't think you're taking my concerns seriously."

"What's wrong?" Jo set aside her silverware and focused her attention on Maxine.

After she pushed back her chair, Maxine strode over to the sofa. She shoved aside a mountain of throw pillows that Jo had purchased over the past week as part of her retail therapy and sank into the cushions, extending her legs across the coffee table. "Every day, I wake up stiff and sore. My skin is dry. My hair is brittle." She lifted a handful of dull-looking strands, which had grayed at the scalp.

Jo strode across the room and sat beside her. She touched her elbow. "Why didn't you tell me?"

"How could I?" Maxine dropped the hair. It fell against

her shoulder like limp spaghetti. "But that's not all. Feel this." With trembling fingers, she grabbed Jo's hand and rubbed it against her cheek. This afternoon, she had felt the coarse sandpaper texture above her lip when she went to scratch beneath her nose.

"Oh my." Jo withdrew her hand. "You're switching."

Tears welled up in Maxine's eyes, and her vision blurred. "I'd rather be dead than become an old man." Her voice hitched.

"No, you wouldn't." Jo wrapped her arms around Maxine's body and squeezed.

"Yes, I would." Maxine wriggled out of the embrace. "I have nothing to look forward to anymore. Patty's dead. My mom disowned me today." She caught her breath and rubbed her eyes with her fists. "I'll never have the career I wanted, working in biotech, like you."

Jo heaved a sigh. "Is that all you want? A job in biotech, like me?"

"Why else did I befriend you last year?" Maxine slapped her hands against her thighs and glowered. "I wasn't looking for a relationship. I was looking for a career." She gulped. "I thought you knew."

"I thought you *liked* me," Jo said. "We had a lot in common with our interest in business." She shifted on the sofa and narrowed her gaze. "So, is that why you haven't talked to me these past few days? You were afraid of switching and losing out on a career?"

Maxine glanced at her feet. Her whole life seemed to shrink down to this moment. Listening to Jo echo her concerns made everything sound petty and inconsequential. Was she that naive to believe those things mattered? Or was she missing the point of life?

Pressure built within her chest, and a sob escaped

from her lips. She buried her head in her hands and cried.

Jo tugged her close and placed her head against her shoulder. She kissed her hair. "I guess, deep down, I suspected the truth. You would throw me away once your career got off to a good start."

"Is that why you never hired me? So you could keep me with you longer?"

"No, that's not why." Jo stroked her arm. "I fell in love with you, and I thought you had fallen in love with me, so none of that mattered anymore. But I was wrong."

Maxine sniffed and rubbed the snot from her face with the back of her hand. "I texted my mom, asking if I could move back, and she disowned me. She told me I had some lessons to learn on my own."

Jo stretched across Maxine's legs and grabbed a handful of tissues from a dispenser on the coffee table. She offered them to Maxine. "Do you want to break up and move out?"

Maxine dabbed her face with the tissues. That had been her initial thought, her first impression, but as she sat next to Jo on the sofa, her head resting next to Jo's chest, she felt something else rise within her—a sense of safety being with the only person who knew how to survive in this evolving world that had turned inside out.

She crumpled the tissues in her fist and thought for a moment longer. "No. I don't. Do you?"

Jo kissed the top of her head again. "I want to be with you forever. However long that is."

CHAPTER 16

That night, Maxine could not sleep. She lay next to Jo and rubbed a suddenly rough, large hand over her five-o'clock shadow. Her chest and back strained against the seams of her nightshirt. She sat up and tugged the shirt over her head. Through the slats in the plantation shutters, the moonlight illuminated the fact that her breasts had hardened and flattened. A few gray hairs sprouted around the nipples. When her toes pinched against her socks, she removed them too.

"Can't sleep?" Jo rolled over and gasped. "Oh my."

The shock in her voice propelled Maxine out of bed. Her legs had thickened, and her center of balance had shifted with the adjustment of the contours of her body. If she moved too quickly, she felt the strain in her muscles. Every motion existed in two timelines—the one in which she imagined the movement and the one in which the movement was accomplished. The discordant space between thought and action unsettled her. Her body no longer responded with ease, but inched along with mysterious aches and pains, much like she'd experienced during adolescence when she could not sleep because her bones were growing.

In the bathroom, Maxine flicked on the lights and grabbed the edge of the sink. Her broad hands were speckled with age spots. Feeling an urgency to urinate, she sat on the toilet seat. Something dangled between her legs, but she was too groggy to care. She released the stream until it tinkled to a stop. With an unsteady hand, she dabbed herself down there before she realized she no longer needed the tissue. Just a shake of her new penis, and she was clean.

Standing, she flushed the toilet and washed her hands. Catching her reflection in the mirror, she understood why Jo had gasped. She looked just like her father before he had died. A wizened old man with a crinkly face; beady, dark brown eyes beneath bushy gray eyebrows; and a bulbous nose. Turning away from her reflection, she dried her hands.

Back in the bedroom, she struggled to get into bed. Her knees were locked.

Jo rushed out from under the covers and padded around the mattress. "Let me help you."

She told Maxine about the time her mother had been ill and how the in-home health aide had shown her how to get her mother to sit on the edge of the bed first before swinging her legs onto the mattress. The two-step process was odd and cumbersome, but with Jo's assistance, Maxine was able to lie down again.

"I look like my dad," Maxine said, her hands folded over her chest. She closed her eyes and whispered, "Dad."

If only she could talk to her father, then maybe everything would be all right.

In the morning, Jo brought Maxine a cup of coffee, sweetened with cream and raw sugar. She sat on the edge of the mattress and patted the back of her hand. "I called in sick to work today," she said. "I don't want to leave you alone. I remember how scared I was when I woke up a woman, and I imagine you must feel the same way, being a man."

Maxine blinked. She struggled to sit propped against the pillows. Her hands shook around the mug. She feared she might spill the hot liquid when she brought it to her lips. The concern in Jo's eyes only spiked her worries. Was she as old as she felt?

"I asked for family leave, but I can't take it." Jo pouted.

"Why not?"

"We're not married."

"Oh." Maxine tried to remember something from one of the courses she had taken about human resource management, but the fact was smooth and slippery, swimming just out of reach.

Maxine drank the coffee and stared at her body. Her chest was flat and broad and muscular and covered with gray tufts of hair. She frowned at her legs, which had grown thick and hairy, next to her oversize feet. "I'm no longer me," she said in a deep, husky voice.

"You're still you," Jo said, squeezing her knee.

Maxine handed Jo the empty mug. With a foreign hand, she pawed the length of her body, wincing at the missing pieces, the breasts and vagina gone, replaced with a penis and a pair of testicles. She scratched her balls, then closed her eyes, wondering what else would change, how different her new life would be as an eighty-year-old man and not a twenty-two-year-old woman.

CHAPTER 17

"You're dealing with grief," the counselor said.

Max, who had once been Maxine, sat on a lumpy, dated sofa that smelled of spilled coffee. They had been coming to this facility for four weeks, courtesy of Jo, who had volunteered to pay for the therapy since Max didn't have insurance.

"It's temporary," Jo had said, "to help you adjust to the transition."

But each day at the outpatient facility failed to provide relief from the ever-present depression that loomed above Max, shadowing their days.

"Depression isn't grief," Max said.

They faced their counselor, a dour-looking woman with bulldog jowls and heavy nurse's shoes, who swiveled from side to side on a squeaky office chair.

The tiny room was painted in warm burgundy and decorated with bright abstract artwork that looked like a child's finger paintings. A sound machine droned by the window, overlooking the parking lot, followed by an expanse of lawn before disappearing into a forest of trees.

The counselor steepled her fingers and said, "Depression is one of the steps of grief. You're mourning several losses—your gender, your youth, and your dreams. The reality of the situation is harsh and unusual. Let yourself feel."

But that was the problem. Max no longer processed feelings the same way they had as a woman. The sensations were still present—a dull ache beneath the breastbone, an acidic churn in the stomach, a tingle at the base of the spine—but they didn't extend throughout their body and take over their life as they once had. The feelings were contained, isolated, boxed up, and stored on an internal shelf so they could go about their day and function without anyone suspecting anything was beneath the surface. The experience left them feeling beside themselves—her, but not her; him, but not him.

Over the weeks, they had changed their name from Maxine to Maximillan—from driver's license to diploma. After losing their job at the delivery service for being a no-show, they had sent their résumé to several headhunters, explaining the odd circumstances, but no one wanted to represent them because no employer wanted to hire an employee who was eligible for Social Security benefits—which Max couldn't collect since they had only recently started to pay into the system, so they had to work or rely on Jo, which somehow seemed so much worse. Old age, like childhood, created dependency. The dynamics had shifted in their relationship with Jo, tipping things out of balance, with all the power in Jo's court and all the helplessness in Max's lap.

"I can't feel the way you want me to feel," Max said. "I'm broken."

"You're not broken. You're metamorphosed," the counselor said with a strained smile.

"Metamorphosed," Max said, thinking of the butterfly fluttering outside the window, darting back and forth, around and around, a flash of white wings.

"Why don't we go meet with others who have metamorphosed?" the counselor suggested.

Max followed the counselor out of the room and down the hall to a conference room, where the chairs were arranged in a circle. They glanced around at the occupants, either old men or young women, and wondered how communing with these patients would help them overcome their depression.

They took a seat in the only chair available.

The young woman beside them offered a hand. "I'm Candy," she said. "But I used to be Candide."

She looked like a sweetheart with a heart-shaped face—high cheekbones and a pointed chin. Her hair was cropped close to her face, and her clothes were structured, almost boxy. She was both masculine and feminine, and the mix suited her.

"I'm Max," they said, shaking her hand. "I used to be Maxine." They didn't know how they looked to her, but they knew how they felt—an imposter, housed in a wrinkled body.

"I don't like being a young woman," Candy said, pouting. "It's hard being the same age as my granddaughter."

She reminded Max of Peter Pan, the boy who never wanted to grow up, which was ironic since Candy not only wanted to be grown up, but she also wanted to be as close to death as possible without dying.

"I don't like being old," Max said, offering a wan smile. Between the joint aches and the memory lapses, they felt like they were spiraling around an open drain, always on the verge of being sucked down.

"But you're okay with being a man?" Candy asked.

Max considered the question for a long while. There were some advantages to having a male body, but Max didn't think of themselves as a man. Max was Maxine. Maxine was Max. A human, trapped in someone else's body. A hostage captured and taken, never to be returned, unless a medical miracle was discovered, which Max doubted would happen during their lifetime.

But Max didn't think Candy wanted this complicated explanation, so they said, "I'm okay with it. I don't have to put on makeup or wear fancy clothes." They scratched their chin. "I can be a slob, and no one cares."

After a brief nod, Candy lowered her gaze. "I miss being an old man. I don't know who I am anymore."

"Me too," Max said, and it was the truth.

That evening, Max opened the front door and caught Jo sitting at the dining room table, scrolling through her phone. A deep line creased between her eyebrows.

A tick of panic pulsed through Max's body. It was early, not even four o'clock, and Max knew Jo didn't make it a habit of coming home before six.

They shuffled over to where she sat and squeezed her shoulder. "Everything okay?"

Without a word, Jo tapped a message on her phone, and a browser loaded with news regarding her company. She pointed to the headlines.

"Is Brain-to-Brain an Invasion of Privacy or Cell Phone Replacement?"

"Big Brother or Big Business—the Consequences of Brain-to-Brain Technology."

She clicked on the first link.

From over her shoulder, Max read the list of pros

and cons, proposed applications, and alleged misuses, including the invasion of privacy. The technology had been suspended by the FCC, but the journalists didn't seem to care.

"So, what does this mean?" Max asked.

Jo fiddled with her phone. "The board fired me."

"What?" Max sank into the nearest chair.

Nodding, Jo placed her phone face down on the table. "We have no new products in development. Our profit share in the industry has collapsed, and as you can see, the failed B2B software has sparked larger concerns, so even if the FCC approved any future revisions to the project, no one would want to market a software that violates personal privacy. It's bad business sense."

The crease between her eyebrows deepened. She splayed her fingers flat against the dining room table.

The nervous gesture triggered a ripple of anxiety.

"How are we going to pay for things?" Max asked. "Will we have to sell the house and move into an apartment?" They glanced around the great room, trying to imagine a space big enough to house all their things.

"Don't worry," Jo said. "I have a plan."

"You do?" A wave of relief washed over them. "What is it?"

Jo seized her phone. "I don't feel like cooking. Do you?"

"You're changing the subject."

"No, I'm ordering Chinese. Chow mein or fried rice."

"Chow mein." Max held their breath, counting backward from ten, just as the counselor had taught them when things didn't go their way.

After Jo placed the order, she closed the app and placed the phone aside. She folded her hands. "The plan is to sell most of my shares and buy Zander's company before they go public."

Max didn't know much about Zander's company. They knew it had something to do with tech—all of Jo's interests did—but other than that, they had no clue. "What do they do?"

"I'm not going to buy them for what they do— warehousing thoughts. I'm going to buy them for what they can do—harness the energy of those warehoused thoughts."

Frowning, Max blew out a forceful exhale. "I don't follow."

Jo unclasped her hands. "Thoughts are energy. If we can harness the energy of warehoused thoughts, then we can provide clean energy to power the world. No more worries about pollution."

"What about privacy issues?" Max imagined the warehoused thoughts couldn't be used for anything while being stored.

"The actual thoughts won't be made public. Their energy will be harnessed to power things. When the consumer wants their thoughts back, we'll give it to them, and the energy needs will be transferred to another set of thoughts someone else has warehoused." Jo waved her hands to mimic the flow of the process. "Eli and my chief neuroscientist, Dr. Dio, have agreed to work on the project if I can get Zander to agree to a sale price."

Max studied the grain on the dining room table. They didn't know much about thought technology, like Jo did, but they did understand the concept of business, and if Jo thought this idea was worth investing in, Max didn't doubt her judgment. "Okay."

"I already have a name for our product," Jo said, the enthusiasm rising in her voice. "Max Pure Energy. Named after you. There's no board of directors, so I could hire you to work as my partner, fifty-fifty, if you're still interested in having a career. What do you say?"

Glancing up, Max met Jo's steady gaze. A fizzy feeling tingled throughout their body. *She would hire me. To work with her.* The prospect sounded appealing.

Max's phone pinged. "Okay. I accept."

"Great." Jo stretched her arm across the table and squeezed Max's hand. "Aren't you going to answer your phone?"

Grunting, Max reached into their breast pocket and removed the device. They swiped a finger across the screen and read a message from their mother. "Patty's family is having a celebration of life for her on my birthday next week. My mom wants me to go."

"I thought you weren't talking with your mother."

"I'm not." Max set the phone on the table.

"Maybe this is a peace offering."

Max snorted. "Hardly. She thinks funerals are one of those obligatory things you do, like pass out candy on Halloween."

"I'll go with you."

"There's nothing to celebrate." Max slapped their palms on the table. "She's dead. It's not my fault we couldn't get to the funeral. There were protests."

"The protests ended weeks ago."

True. Max imagined it was because everyone who had transitioned was too busy adjusting to their new life to complain about it.

Jo squeezed Max's hand. "Go out of respect."

"You sound like my mother."

The doorbell rang.

"Go set the table. I'll get the food." Jo stood to answer

the door.

Max reluctantly obeyed. Even with the partnership agreement, they felt like a child, lesser than, diminished. When would they feel empowered and capable? They shuffled to the cabinets, taking down plates, gathering silverware, and stooped to arrange everything on the end of the dining room table that Jo didn't use as her home office.

Jo unboxed the cartons of chow mein, sweet and sour pork, and lemon chicken. The cacophony of scents mingled into a dense mist, reminding Max of the lazy dinners her mother used to make. They missed the elaborate dishes Jo used to make, like beef wellington or chicken cordon bleu, but lately, she served only American basics, like bowls of chili with cut-up hot dogs and macaroni and cheese, when she wasn't ordering takeout. Maybe Max would have to learn how to cook.

After taking a seat, Max snapped apart a pair of takeout chopsticks. They served up chow mein and sweet and sour pork on their plate, skipping the lemon chicken.

"I don't ask much of you." Jo slapped a mound of sweet and sour pork onto her plate. Her voice rose. "Please, go to Patty's service." She flared her nostrils.

Max grunted. They knew Jo was right. She didn't ask Max for anything. They didn't have to work, clean the house, pay the bills, or garden in the yard. They didn't even have to have sex. Not that Max wanted sex. The desire had leaked away. The counselor had said it was a common symptom of depression, but Max suspected old age had something to do with it.

Jo sighed and placed her hand on Max's wrist. "I'm sorry for my anger." She swallowed and bowed her head. "I'm just disappointed in your behavior. You're acting like a spoiled child and not a grown man." Her voice hitched. "I thought we should attend."

Nodding, Max squeezed her fingers. But they didn't want to go, not alone and not with Jo, because attendance at the service meant acknowledging death, and that was something Max refused to do. Growing old was hard enough. Death was impossible.

"Is your mom attending?" Jo withdrew her hand and raised a mouthful of sweet and sour pork to her lips.

"Of course." Max shook their head. "I haven't told her I've switched."

"You should."

Nodding, Max fiddled with their chopsticks. If they attended the celebration of life, they wouldn't have to tell their mother anything. She would know. "I really don't want to do anything."

"Therapy's not helping, is it?"

Max shrugged. They didn't like the prospect of Jo losing money, but they didn't want to lie.

"You can quit anytime."

Max imagined the vacancy of their days stretching out listlessly before them. They could fill the time— maybe take a cooking course or two, learn how to garden, try out yoga to lengthen their achy limbs. But they would miss the one person who they had come to associate with hope—Candy. Unlike Jo, Candy didn't relish the opportunity to be young again, to relive her life with the benefit of wisdom. She mourned the loss of her old age as powerfully as Max mourned the loss of youth. What would they do without their new friend?

Jo sighed. "I can talk to your counselor."

"No, don't." Max didn't want Jo parenting their life. "I'll talk to her." They fiddled with their noodles. "I have made a friend. That's helping, so I think I'll go for a little while longer, if you don't mind."

"Of course. I want you to get better."

"I just don't want to get to the end of my life without having lived, you know?"

Jo sighed. "No one knows how long we have. We only have this moment. That's why it's called the present."

Max chuckled at the crappy, corny platitude. "You suck as a motivational speaker."

"That's not all I suck at." Jo raised her eyebrows and slanted a smile, her fingers inching across the back of Max's hand.

The joke was not lost on Max. They tried to ignore the slow burn fanning across the center of their body.

Jo lifted Max's hand and brought it to her lips. She kissed each knuckle, her gaze never wavering from their face.

The flame lapped into a fire, and Max dropped the chopsticks from their other hand.

Jo rose from the chair and stepped back from the table.

Max stood, yielding to a silent, burning yearning, as they followed Jo the bedroom at the other end of the house.

CHAPTER 18

Max sat across from the counselor in the burgundy office. They stared at the view of the parking lot while listening to the same drivel they listened to every day without feeling one ounce better about their condition or their life.

"The first step toward acceptance is to look unflinchingly at reality," the counselor said. She leaned forward in the squeaky chair, crossing her ankles, her feet in those clunky black nurse's shoes. "Repeat after me: *I am an old man.*"

Max dug their nails into the palm of their hand. "I am an old man," they said.

"Again," the counselor said. "With *feeling* this time."

"I am an old man!"

"Better," the counselor said. "But try it again without the anger. Go for acceptance."

Sighing, Max uncurled their hands on their lap, palms up, like the statue of the Buddha in the meditation room, next to the conference room where group therapy was held. They inhaled deeply for a count of four, held for a count of seven, and exhaled for a count of eight.

"I am an old man." The words rolled off the tongue, somnolent and dreamy, the closest they could get to the truth.

"That's it." The counselor uncrossed her ankles and smiled. "Now repeat after me: *This is my life. I have no other.*"

But Max didn't want this old man to be their life. They wanted another life, another body, another option. Saying these things—*I am not an old man. This is not my life. I have another*—would only double down on the counselor's efforts to convince them otherwise. But what use were these mantras and affirmations? They roiled around their consciousness like fill-in-the-blank answers to an exam that had nothing to do with real life.

"Max?" The counselor frowned, leaning forward. "What's the problem?"

The problem was beyond articulation. Max rubbed their eyes until their vision blurred. Only then did they feel better with everything out of focus.

"This is my life," they said. "I have no other." The words fell from their lips like weighted balls clunk-clunking at their feet.

That feeling of being trapped without an escape returned, and Max rubbed their eyes again, hoping the cloudy, misty vision would ease the pain.

But that pain didn't lift until group therapy began. Max sat next to Candy, as always, in the circle of people who had transitioned against their will. Today, Candy wore a bronze halter top, black leggings, and sneakers.

When she caught Max staring, she said, "My granddaughter dressed me today."

Nodding, Max wondered how their grandfather would have dressed them if he had been alive. The memories they had were patchy—an olive-green button-down shirt, a belted pair of black slacks, and loafers, polished to a shine. A heated shame brushed across their face, and they crossed their arms, as if the gesture could cross out the stained T-shirt and sweatpants, which were so long that they bunched at the ankles. Both articles of clothing had been borrowed from Jo's old wardrobe.

"You look about my size," Candy said. "I could give you my old clothes if you want to dress better."

"Yes, please," Max said, wondering what Candy might have worn when she was Candide.

When it was time to go around the circle and share, Max volunteered new information instead of rehashing the same complaints. "My girlfriend wants me to attend my best friend's celebration of life, but I don't want to go."

"Why not?" the counselor asked.

Max stared at a speck of lint on the industrial-grade gray carpet. "I don't want to think about dying."

Candy scooted closer—so close that she brushed against Max's arm. "All my friends died before the switch started. Now I'm faced with trying to make friends with people my granddaughter's age. It's discombobulating."

Max laughed at the weird word. "Discom—what?"

"Discombobulating. It means confusing."

That was exactly how Max felt. Discombobulated.

After group therapy ended, Max walked Candy to the lobby and exchanged phone numbers. They needed someone who understood what it felt like to be in a body that felt as foreign as being dropped in the middle of a country where no one spoke the only language you knew. How could you navigate the situation, get what you needed, and go where you wanted to go?

"I'm not working right now," Max said. "I could pick you up and take you to therapy."

Candy glanced at the young woman who had strolled

across the lobby. She was taller than Candy but shared the same face structure and lanky limbs.

"Thanks, but I promised my daughter that Sarah could take me. Gives my granddaughter something constructive to do. You know?"

Max didn't know. They didn't have a daughter or a granddaughter, but they did need something constructive to do. "Okay. But call if you change your mind."

"Will do." Candy nodded at Sarah. "Ready?"

Max studied them standing side by side. A stranger would not have known which one had metamorphized and which one had been born that way unless they stared into the eyes a bit too long—for Candy's gaze held a gleam of age-related fatigue and wisdom that Sarah lacked. But most people didn't pay attention, so they would never guess the awkwardness of being part of a social circle where they were never meant to belong. But Max empathized with Candy and her situation. If they could have swapped places, they would have, even though they didn't particularly favor Candy's heart-shaped face and bone-thin body. Any young female body was better than the old male body Max had.

Max strode outside with them and stood by their car while Candy and her granddaughter drove away. They remained outside their sedan, staring at the vacant space the vehicle had once occupied. The peculiar heat of September blazed against their forehead, and a stream of perspiration caught in the folds of their chin. They stayed standing and staring so long that they didn't see or hear the counselor padding up to them, asking if they were all right. The voice sounded as distant as birdsong.

"Max?" The counselor touched their arm. "Are you

all right? Do I need to call 911? You might be having a stroke."

Max blinked, glancing down at the hand resting on their forearm. "I'm fine," they said. "I was thinking. That's all." Why couldn't they mull over a situation without someone's concern? "I just want to be left alone. Thank you."

"Staring can sometimes indicate a mini stroke," the counselor said. "I would prefer if you came inside and let one of the nurses on staff examine you."

"I'm *fine*." The venom stung in their voice. They unlocked the car door and slipped inside. "I'll see you next week." They started the engine, rolled down the windows halfway, and turned up the air-conditioning to combat the swollen heat.

"I'm fine," they repeated, shifting into reverse and backing up.

They noticed the counselor, slack-jawed and immobile, in the rearview mirror as they drove across the parking lot and turned onto the main street.

"I'm fine." They repeated the sentence over and over, as if the act of repetition alone would make it true.

Max knew Jo was good at business, but didn't know how good she was until she announced a contract had been drawn up and approved by both parties within days of announcing her decision to acquire Zander's company.

"We close at the end of the week and start work on Monday," she said that night at dinner.

"Congratulations." Max raised their glass of water and clicked to the toast.

On Monday, Max commuted with Jo to the new office, tucked at the end of a cul-de-sac that backed to an abandoned railroad track. The stark oak trees towered over the squat beige building, which was modest compared to the large industrial-park feel of Jo's old corporation. Even the lobby was unimpressive with a laminate floor and a simple receptionist desk behind a wall of Plexiglas. One narrow hallway led to all the offices and ended at a doorway opening to the warehouse, where most of the staff worked. The cavernous space reminded Max of the old manufacturing buildings they had studied in warehouse operations management. The steel beam ceilings stretched three stories high with aisle upon aisle of computers stacked up like towers. Employees scurried up and down the rows of housed thoughts, monitoring the inventory. Max didn't know what else they could be doing or why.

Jo promised to soften the entire operation with feminine touches from her new habit of retail shopping that Max suspected was a little out of control, judging by the proliferation of throw pillows everywhere in the house they shared. But Max didn't complain—couldn't complain. They had no money, no experience, only education, and education alone wasn't enough to veto experience and money.

Back in the main building, they settled into the space between Jo's and Eli's offices. They had a sleek black desk, a standard office chair, a laptop, a bookcase, and two visitor chairs poised on the opposite side of the black desk. Across from the door, a window looked out at the abandoned railroad tracks beneath the shade of the oak trees.

They didn't know what their job entailed, but they didn't mind waiting for instructions from Jo. At least, they were here, being productive, rather than at home, moping about and pining for their old body, their old life, their old dreams. Sure, they struggled to get up out of the office chair, scooting to the edge of the seat and grasping the ledge of the desk to stand in two motions —out, then up. And their typing speed was slow, more like a hen pecking at the keys than the smooth dance of fingers across the keyboard. And their mind, once sharp and nearly photographic, inched through empty cabinets of information before plucking the right word to describe a fact, opinion, or memory.

But what bothered Max the most was watching Eli interact with Jo. He was always striding past their office to Jo's, clicking the door closed, talking in a low, hushed voice, like everything was a secret. Once in a while, Jo's laughter pealed through the walls, startling Max with its ebullience. A rod of fear steeled their back, and they wondered if the benign friendship between coworkers was something else. Maybe the start of a flirtatious attraction.

"We're just talking business," Jo said every time Max asked.

"But you sound happy."

"I am happy. I'm working on something new, something no one has done before, and I'm confident we'll have a product ready for release by this time next year."

But Jo's reassurances did nothing to quell the uneasiness of witnessing Eli's swagger in the hallway, his way of tossing back his hair when he laughed at one of

Jo's inane jokes, or the glint of mischief in his brown eyes whenever he proposed a suggestion during meetings about research and development. He was nothing like the unassuming geeky man, hiding behind a scruffy beard and baggy clothes, who Max had first met over a year ago. He was confident and cocky, thrusting his bare chin forward, puffing out his chest, and speaking his truth with a booming voice that matched his new demeanor.

The only thing worse was Jo's reaction to Eli's behavior. She strained forward, crossing her legs and leaning toward him, the cleavage rising against the unbuttoned collar of her blouse, nodding in agreement or tilting her head to the side in wonder or screwing her lips in concentration or shaking her head in disagreement. Was the spark in her eyes truly just business? Or was it something else, something physical?

Was Jo falling for Eli, and he for her?

"I think you're overreacting," Candy said when Max called to take her out to lunch to talk.

They sat across the street from the office, in an outdoor café, beneath an umbrella to deflect the afternoon sunlight, eating ham and cheese sandwiches with their chips and sodas. Crisp red and golden leaves, blown from the branches of the old oak trees, scuttled across their feet.

"What would you do?" Max said between chews.

"Nothing," Candy said. She fluttered her hands like wings. "I think you should drop it. Coworkers joke and flirt all the time. It's part of the office chemistry. I'd only be concerned if the relationship stretched beyond working hours."

Max leaned back against the seat and crossed their arms over their chest. They didn't believe the relationship was innocent, but how could they prove otherwise?

In therapy, which Max continued to attend once a week, they confided their concerns to the counselor, who validated Max's feelings.

"I would talk to Jo and express your concerns," the counselor said.

"I already have. She thinks I'm just insecure and jealous."

"Are you?" The counselor tipped back in her chair, raising her toes in her nurse's shoes.

"I'm sure it looks that way to an outsider," Max said, staring out the window at the parking lot. The afternoon sunlight slanted across the rooftops of the cars, casting glaring shards of sunlight through the slats of the blinds. "But I'm not. I know what flirting looks like. I know what attraction is." They cut their gaze across the counselor's face and clenched their hands into fists. Leaning forward, they spat, "I know danger when I see it."

Without anyone else to confide in, Max retreated, both at work and at home. Once, they considered texting their mother and asking for her advice. But what good would it do? Their mother was paranoid, always seeking darkness in a situation, and her opinion would only fan the flames burning like indigestion in their chest.

CHAPTER 19

On the morning of Patty's celebration of life, Max sat at the foot of the bed, watching Jo gaze at her reflection in the bathroom mirror, frowning at the fake diamond studs in her lobes. She had recently pierced her ears at Max's suggestion, and the skin had not healed enough for her to wear the pearls she had bought for the occasion.

"You look fine," Max said, wishing she didn't have a habit of tugging on her lobes whenever she was nervous. They didn't know why she was concerned. Patty had been primarily their friend, not hers.

Jo braced her arms against the counter and bowed her head. "Don't mind me."

"That time of the month?" Max didn't miss the surge of hormones coursing through their body—the cramps, the headaches, the food cravings, the sexual yearnings. But they did miss other things—the familiarity and comfort of knowing oneself.

Lifting her head, Jo met Max's gaze through her reflection. She ran a hand across her stomach. "I feel strange."

"Strange?"

"Nauseous."

Max grunted. "Maybe the expiration date on the food

we ate last night was wrong."

They bunched their fists on either side of their hips and hoisted to standing. Their joints crackled, and a static of pain zigzagged down their legs. They shook their feet, one after the other, and hobbled over to the bathroom to stand side by side with Jo. With their hands, they smoothed down the black suit they had received from Candy. All the donated clothes fit, almost perfectly, as if the two of them were—or had been—the same size. When Max had offered their clothes to Candy, she had declined, citing it would cause a fight with her granddaughter, who preferred to be the one dressing her.

"No, I don't think it's that." But she didn't say what she thought it was. She only blinked and asked, "Are you nervous?"

"My mom will be there." Max allowed Jo to straighten their tie, which had been one of hers when she was a man, which seemed a lifetime ago, even though it had only been several months.

"It would be good for you to talk with her."

"She doesn't know I'm different now."

"After today, she will."

Max grunted again. They didn't need any more problems.

"By the way, happy birthday, love." Jo pecked Max on the lips.

The loving touch fizzled into annoyance. *Not another birthday.*

When Maxine had been in her twenties, she had looked forward to becoming twenty-one. Eighty-one seemed a ridiculous amount of time to celebrate.

But Max didn't want to crush Jo's heart, so they folded her in their arms and breathed in the scent of her floral perfume. "Thanks."

The drive to the country club, where the celebration would take place, didn't take long. The protests that had once clogged the roads died away months ago, and the statewide curfew had been lifted for a few weeks. Most people affected by the switch had metamorphized, so it wasn't a big deal anymore.

In the parking lot, Max spotted their mother's car. They braced their back against the seat, taking big gulps of air, trying to steady their nerves, but the same chorus of thoughts circulated in their mind. *My mother never accepted me. Why would she accept me now? I should have stayed home.*

"Ready?"

The question, coupled with the proximity of being two cars away from their mother's sedan, was enough to spark a series of gulps and gasps.

"What's wrong?" Jo grabbed Max's hand across the console and squeezed their fingers.

The jolt of their heartbeat pounding against their chest sounded like a stampede of wild animals in their ears. A flurry of perspiration dotted the top of their bald head, and Max used the handkerchief in their breast pocket to dab the moisture away with shaking hands. "I can't—"

"Yes, you can." Jo squeezed encouragement into their fingers. "I'll be right next to you."

"But you can't stop my mother from saying horrible things about you and me and our relationship."

"Who cares?"

"I do." Max closed their eyes and took a handful of deep breaths, counting like the counselor had taught them, but the fear continued to bob inside them. "I don't want her to see me this way." They gulped. "I look like my father."

"Is that a bad thing?" Jo sighed, still rubbing their fingers. "Your father must have been an attractive man if you look like him."

Max laughed until they snorted. They were bald and tubby, like a life-sized egg. They shook their fingers loose from Jo's grip and bundled them into their lap. "I don't want to keep disappointing her. I wasn't good enough as a woman. What makes you think I'll be acceptable as a man?"

Jo stared at her nails. "Do you want to stay in the car while I pay my respects?"

The autumn air still held the heat of summer, and Max imagined they would be nothing but a pool of sweat if left inside to rot while Jo mingled. "No, I'll come, but I won't stay long."

"Deal." Jo stepped outside and held the door open for Max.

Together, they walked, arm in arm, into the cool air-conditioning of the country club, where old men gathered with young men to drink beer and chat about what had happened since graduation.

Max glanced at the crowd, noticing a handful of people, but refused to mingle.

"Thanks for coming," said a young woman who looked a lot like Patty. "I'm glad you could make it."

"Sure, no problem," Max said, offering to shake the young woman's hand. "I'm Maxine, Patty's best friend."

"I'm Patty's dad," the young woman said, accepting the handshake.

"And this is my partner, Jo." Max nodded to Jo, who flashed a warm smile.

"My pleasure," Patty's dad said, shaking Jo's hand. "I'm Rick. I go by Ricki now. Like the late great Ricki Lake. Remember her?"

"The talk show host," Jo said, laughing. "My grandmother used to watch her when I was a kid."

"Mine, too," Ricki said.

Max, not knowing or caring about who Ricki Lake was, meandered over to the gathering of men on the other side of the room. They passed a table full of beer and snacks and paused at a guest book, laid open with a pen. For a long moment, Max thought about writing something sweet and profound, but the words wouldn't come. Everything they felt was lodged deep beneath the skin, as deep as the cellular level, where energy crisscrossed back and forth through semipermeable membranes, communicating through the exchange of chemical-like signals. They glanced around the room, at the old men who had once been young women, to the young men who remained the same, to the photograph of Patty on a pedestal, surrounded by a halo of white roses. That photo had been taken in high school, not college, and the hopeful smile on Patty's lips belied the quiet desperation Max felt.

"Why you and not me?" they asked, staring at the photo.

Although the room was big and airy with vaulted ceilings, painted white as the clouds, Max felt boxed in, claustrophobic, like the people milling about were the sides of a trash compactor moving toward them. Through the crowd of guests, they looked for signs of their mother, but they did not see any women present.

"They're inside the chapel," one of the men said, pointing to the white double doors. "They're setting up the microphone for those of us who want to share stories about Patty."

Max nodded, grateful for the information. When the double doors opened, they moved against the crowd, away from the chapel. Escaping down a hallway, they leaned against a wall beneath an air-conditioning vent that blasted freezing air against their sweaty face. They gulped back huge mouthfuls of sorrow until they hiccuped. The spasm built from the chest and spouted upward into a squeaky sound escaping from their mouth. Suddenly, Max wished they were back in the conference room at the outpatient treatment center, sitting next to Candy, who would somehow know what to do in this situation since all her friends had already died and she had finished with her mourning. But Max was here, alone and lonely, not there.

Jo was in the other room, probably still chatting with Patty's father, and for the first time since the switch, Max wondered what life would look like without anyone they had ever known. The thought didn't last long because Jo rounded the corner in her click-clack heels and touched their elbow.

"Ready to go?"

Max gulped, swallowing a hiccup. "Yes."

Outside, in the abnormal heat, Jo looped her arm through Max's and asked, "Did you see your mother?"

"No, but all the women were in the chapel."

"Ah, that explains why you were in the other room." Jo matched Max's slow shuffle. "So, I guess inviting your mom to your birthday dinner is out of the question."

"Right." Max opened the car door. Holding on to the doorframe, they lowered themselves onto the warm leather seat. The effort left them breathless.

"Are you okay?" Jo leaned forward, her pearl necklace dangling near Max's face.

"I'm fine," Max lied.

While Jo drove, Max leaned their head against the back of the seat and closed their eyes. The cool air blowing from the vents wicked away the moisture from their face. "I hope you don't have any surprises for my birthday."

"Just dinner with a friend."

"Candy?" Max snapped open their eyes. "How did you get her number?"

Jo kept her gaze on the road, but she jutted her chin toward Max. "Go ahead and call her. We're meeting Eli at The Cabana at six." Stopping at a light, she tapped her fingers against the steering wheel. "I was hoping your mother would join us."

Max slipped their phone out of their breast pocket and sent a thought-to-text to Candy. "I'm not ready to see my mother."

Within moments, Max's phone pinged with a response. They swiped their finger across the screen. Candy agreed to attend their birthday dinner. A smile warmed Max's face. They tucked their phone back into their breast pocket.

"Candy's coming."

"Good." A muscle twitched in Jo's cheek.

Max twisted their hands together. "Why don't you like Candy?"

"I never said I didn't like Candy." Jo fixed her gaze at Max. "I don't know her."

The pitch of Jo's voice made it sound like she was jealous of the competition. Max bit their lower lip, stanching a tirade of comebacks that would only fuel the uncomfortable situation.

"I'm sorry," Jo said, flicking the indicator to turn down their street. "I guess I'm a little worried about how much you like this woman I've never met."

"Don't be. You'll meet her tonight. You probably have more in common with her than I do."

Jo snorted. "Just because she used to be a man?"

A prickle of heat brushed across Max's face.

Jo steered the sports car into the garage and turned off the engine. The tick-tick-tick of the motor filled the silence.

She grabbed her purse and popped open the door. "Are you coming? Or are you sulking in the car for the next two hours?"

Max swung the door wide and grabbed the frame, hoisting their body to standing. They shuffled a couple of steps, then slammed the door closed.

"Are you angry?" Jo paused on the second step leading into the house and punched the button to activate the garage door. The panels rattled across the steel frame and swallowed the room in stifling darkness.

"Not more than you are." Max seized the railing and maneuvered up the two steps into the cool house.

They padded after Jo, who flung her purse on the sofa and kicked off her heels under the coffee table on her way toward the bedroom. They loomed in the doorway, glaring at the disarray of clothing on the bed and the floor as Jo finished disrobing.

After strutting to the walk-in closet in nothing but a bra and underwear, Jo flicked through the racks of blouses, slacks, skirts, and dresses before selecting a peach-colored wrap dress and matching heels. She slipped into the new dress, then sank onto a bench she had purchased and rubbed her bare feet before slipping them into the heels.

Nodding to Max, she asked, "You wearing that suit to dinner?"

Max bent to pick up the black dress that had slipped from the bed to the floor. Their balance wobbled, and they leaned against the dresser to orient themselves. They grabbed a wire hanger and hung the dress next to a navy-blue blazer in the lineup of color-coordinated clothing. They twisted their hands together, trying to puzzle out what they wanted to say without offending Jo any further.

"Eli is not my friend."

"Is that why you're upset? Because I invited Eli to dinner?" Jo stood and towered over Max. "He's *our* friend, just like Patty was our friend."

"He's *in love* with you."

Jo gasped. "He *is not*."

"Yes, he *is*."

"Not."

"Is."

"Never. I work with him. We've known each other for years."

"But he's only known you as a man. A father figure. Now you're younger than him. And a very attractive woman." Max inhaled. The air caught in their chest, and they coughed.

Jo waved her hand. "And this Candy woman—how is she different from Eli? How do I know she doesn't have feelings for you? Or you for her?"

Max wagged their head from side to side. They hadn't fought with anyone this much since they'd moved out of their mother's house. The emotion roiled beneath their skin, heating them into a frenzy, and they struggled to catch their breath. After sinking onto the bench in the walk-in closet, they bent their head and braced their hands on their knees. The weakness in their lungs seemed to mirror the powerlessness they felt in their relationship with Jo.

A trill sounded from inside Max's breast pocket.

They removed their cell phone and swiped on the screen.

—*Where are you? Aren't you coming? The ceremony is almost over.*—

A grim line stretched across Max's face. Their mother. Reprimanding them for not showing up when they had been there just minutes ago. But indistinguishable from all the other guests now that they were no longer a young woman. They palmed the phone, and tears blurred their eyes.

"What's wrong?" Jo stepped into the closet and placed a hand on Max's back. She leaned over, tapped the screen on the phone, and read the message. "You can tell her you were there. Invite her to dinner."

"Or you can cancel dinner," Max said. "I'd rather be alone."

Jo squeezed Max's shoulder. "You spend too much time alone."

"I'm never alone." They held up a hand and counted. "I'm with you at home. I'm with you at work. I'm with you right now. The only time I'm not with you is at therapy. And then I'm with the counselor and other patients like Candy." They curled their fingers into a fist. "I am never alone." They broke down into another coughing fit.

Jo rushed out of the closet and returned a few moments later with a glass of water. "Here."

Max eyed the glass for a long moment before taking a

sip. The cool fluid slipped down their throat and eased the irritation.

"Maybe we should take you to the doctor."

"No doctors." Max didn't want anyone examining them. They didn't want to know what was wrong with their body—a body they had never wanted, but somehow had, a body that kept them guessing, a body that was inevitably falling apart, like a used car. "I just want to lie down and go to sleep." *And never wake up again.*

"That's why I can't afford to have you spend any time alone," Jo said, kneeling before them. "You're depressed. Maybe even suicidal."

Max studied Jo's facial expression. Her eyebrows pinched together. Her lips were drawn in a tight line. The concern was evident and touching.

Max drank another mouthful of water and handed her the glass. "You can hear my thoughts."

"Sometimes." Jo's expression shifted. Her gaze averted toward the carpeting. A swallow moved along the length of her throat.

"I thought you had uninstalled the software."

"I did." She met their gaze. "But Dr. Dio thinks the program embeds into the neural pathways and becomes part of the brain's structure, even after it's uninstalled."

A ghost program. Running in the background. A rogue situation with no solution. No wonder Jo had been fired. Max marveled that the FCC hadn't been alerted. But maybe Eli didn't know. Or was so infatuated with Jo that he had promised to keep a secret for a change. Either way, Max didn't like this new information. The prospect of losing all privacy spiked another surge of hostility.

"Why can't I hear your thoughts?" they asked.

"I don't know."

Max studied Jo's face. Maybe she was telling the truth. Maybe she was lying to protect them. Either way, Max wouldn't know until they cornered Dr. Dio at work and had a conversation.

"So, how about dinner?" Jo rubbed a hand across Max's knees. "You don't have to invite your mom. We can have her over some other time."

Never.

"Or never." Jo shrugged. "It's up to you, okay?"

Nodding, Max was suddenly more afraid to think than they were afraid to say anything aloud.

CHAPTER 20

The hostess led Max and Jo to an outside table by the pool. The stone patio absorbed the heat from earlier in the day, and the setting sun cast long streams of amber light through the slats of the pergola. Between the warmth of the tiles and the coolness from the pool, the conflicting mix of temperatures mirrored the flux of emotions stirring within Max.

"Happy birthday!" The hostess winked, handing Max a menu.

"Thank you." Max forced a smile.

The ambiance—from the tinkling fountain in the pool to the light chatter of conversations—melted the tension in Max's shoulders. Cabana was their favorite restaurant from the moment they had stepped onto the patio over a year ago when Jo took them here for their first official date. They'd sat at the table behind Jo, a two-person affair, where another couple dined tonight, their hands interlinked, their faces just inches apart.

Beyond that table, Max could view the rest of the outdoor dining area and the parking lot, where they spied Eli marching with purposeful steps while struggling to button his tan-colored jacket. A familiar two-door sedan swerved in front of him, missing him by a few feet. The passenger door opened, and Candy slipped out of the idling vehicle.

Her voice carried on the breeze. "Slow down. You almost hit that nice young man."

Max didn't hear the driver's response, but they did notice how Eli stopped to talk to Candy. He even smiled and held the door of the restaurant open for her. A few moments later, the two of them arrived, striding side by side, led by the same hostess who had seated Max and Jo.

Candy, flushed and breathless, bent to hug the sitting Max. "Happy birthday, you old geezer." She chuckled. "Don't look so glum. You know I was your age just months ago. Nothing wrong with getting older."

"As long as you get wiser," Eli said, taking a seat next to Jo.

Candy pulled back the remaining chair next to Max. She held out her hand to Jo. "I'm Candy."

She wore a skimpy dress with spaghetti straps and strappy heels. Probably another outfit put together by her granddaughter. The hair around her face had grown and now curled around her ears, giving her an elfish look.

Jo swept her gaze up and down the length of Candy's body and flashed a tight smile. "Good to finally meet you. I'm Jo, Max's girlfriend." She lifted her chin, defiant and sophisticated in her tasteful peach-colored wrap dress and matching heels, her makeup artfully accentuating her bright eyes, her slender nose, and her blossom-like lips. A telltale wisp of her floral perfume delicately scented the air.

"We already met," Eli said, nodding.

"In the parking lot." Candy grimaced and shook her head. "I told my granddaughter to slow down, but she never listens. I need to look into getting my license renewed. I let it go when I turned seventy. It's been a while since I've been behind the wheel, but I swear I drive better than she ever has."

"Happy birthday, Maxi." Eli removed a card from the inside pocket of his jacket. "Go ahead and open it."

"Later," Max said, feeling the edge of the paper. "Let's order first."

While everyone bowed their heads to peruse the menu, Max excused themselves to use the restroom. In the hallway of the too-warm restaurant, Max glanced from the women's sign to the men's sign. An uncomfortable conundrum rose within as they considered the alternatives. If they entered the men's room, they would be welcomed for their body, but if they entered the women's room, they might feel more comfortable, but they would also attract unwanted attention. Max shuddered, wishing for those days when they didn't have to think of other people's reactions. Men's room it was.

At the sink, washing their hands, they glimpsed the fatigue around their eyes in the mirror. The sadness seemed pervasive, almost like an odor, and for a moment, they wondered if they could just dip out of the whole affair and order a ride home. But they knew both Candy and Eli had a view of the parking lot, so they couldn't escape undetected. Reluctantly, they smoothed the collar of the blue golf shirt Jo had bought as a birthday present and shuffled back to the table, where the server stood, taking the order.

Jo leaned forward, her gaze bright and eager. "I thought you'd like the special, hon. Calamari steak."

"You're right." Max lowered their body into the plush chair. "Thank you."

"You're welcome, hon."

Jo's wide, warm smile made Max's toes tingle. Maybe celebrating their birthday wasn't such a bad idea.

As soon as the server left, Jo turned to Candy. "So, tell us what you do."

Eli touched the back of Jo's hand. "Wait. Shouldn't Maxi open her gift?"

The casual gesture, a light brush of skin against skin, ignited a flare of jealousy in the pit of Max's stomach. They curled their fingers over the envelope. *My name is Max. And I use they/them pronouns.* The thoughts hovered just above their tongue, but they bit back the words.

"I can open it while you talk."

"No, it's your day." Eli straightened his spine. "Let's focus on you."

But how could Max focus on anything other than Eli with his perfect brown curls and big brown eyes and freshly shaved cheeks that smelled like he had splashed half a bottle of cologne on his face? He was dressed in a casual suit, button-down shirt and slacks, and that tailored jacket that made his shoulders look broader and his chest look stronger. Max didn't need a mirror to know how they looked in comparison—a shriveled raisin next to a ripe, juicy grape.

"Fine." Jo tucked her hands into her lap and gazed at Max. "Ready whenever you are, hon."

They wished Jo would stop saying hon. At home, she only used that term of endearment sparingly, lovingly. Tonight, the word sounded jarring and demeaning, punctuating every sentence, like a stab with a sharp knife. But Max decided they would refrain from bringing it up, especially with company. Silently, they ripped the envelope open and tugged out the card.

A cartoon vulture was perched at the top of a

mountain with the caption: *Look at You. A Year Older.* Inside, Eli had written: *Happy birthday from your friendly vulture.*

Max set aside the card without a laugh.

Candy plucked it from the table, read the words, and chuckled. "Funny, Eli." She handed the card to Jo.

After a quick read, Jo gasped. "Eli, how could you? Not everyone shares your sense of humor."

Eli shrugged. "Most people don't get us tech guys." He nodded to Max. "But you should understand, being with Jo and all."

"I think you should apologize," Jo said, narrowing her gaze at Eli.

"No way," Candy said. "It's funny. Max needs to laugh a little." She tugged her purse into her lap and rummaged inside, searching for something. "Ah, here it is." She slid a small package across the table. "Here's something to cheer you up. No joke included."

Max stared at the gift. The box was the perfect size for jewelry. Max gulped. Was Candy gifting an earring? They didn't want a piercing, like Candy's granddaughter had.

"It won't bite," Candy said. "Promise."

Max tugged at the glossy golden paper. Inside the box was a set of sterling silver cuff links, engraved with Max's initials.

"I hope you like them." Candy smiled. "My parents always said every man needs a set of cuff links."

"Thank you." Max removed a cuff link and examined it beneath the fairy lights strung through the wooden beams of the pergola. The silver gleamed. It was a thoughtful gift, a heartfelt one, even if it was a little old-fashioned. They smiled. "How sweet."

Jo cleared her throat and tapped her spoon against the

side of her water glass. "Toast?"

Max carefully placed the cuff link in the box. They raised their water glass.

"To Max," Jo said, lifting her glass. "Happy birthday to the best person I know."

"Hear, hear," Eli said, clicking his glass against the others.

"I'm glad I met you," Candy said. "I'd still be moping around with my granddaughter, feeling sorry for myself, if we'd never met."

Jo sneered. "Max is *still* moping."

"Not as much," Candy said, leveling her gaze at Jo.

For a moment, Max expected a fight.

But a server stopped by with their salads.

As everyone ate, Max glanced from face to face. These people wouldn't be gathered in the same place at the same time if it wasn't their birthday. Max marveled over how anyone could celebrate their existence when they questioned it every day. A pinch of guilt squeezed their chest. Maybe they shouldn't question everything. Maybe they should "roll with it," like their counselor often said.

Candy speared a tomato. "To answer your earlier question, I manage The Spirit Store."

Jo frowned with a forkful of lettuce in midair. "Isn't that a seasonal job?"

Candy lifted one shoulder. "Keeps me busy while I figure out my life." She set her fork against the plate. "I was getting ready to call the curtain when this happened." She fiddled with the napkin on her lap. "I never imagined having to relive my entire adult life. Just thinking of redoing the next sixty years is exhausting."

"I never thought of that," Eli said. He met Candy's gaze across the table.

Max noticed his pupils were dilated. Was he attracted to Candy?

Candy bowed her head and looked up at him with a meaningful gaze. "No one prepares you to live twice."

Jo cleared her throat again. "Yes, well, I'm taking it as an opportunity to do everything I didn't the first time."

"Such as?" Candy asked, lifting her head.

"Well, I've only mentioned this once to Max, but I'd like to have a family someday." Jo raised the corner of her lips in a half smile.

Max choked on a lungful of air. They thought the baby had been a fleeting thought, triggered by monthly hormones, and not a lasting desire. They covered their mouth with a cloth napkin until the coughing stopped.

Eli handed them a glass of water.

Grateful, Max took a sip. A few droplets dribbled from their mouth. They dabbed their lips. Narrowing their gaze at Jo, they said, "I'm too old to have a baby."

"No, you're not." Jo glanced around the table. "Al Pacino was eighty-three when he had his last child." She nodded. "Men stay fertile forever."

Glancing away, Max noticed a toddler sitting in a high chair three tables away. The child banged his fists against the tray and gurgled a bunch of nonsense. The adults cooed and awed in response to the gibberish.

Jo's fingers touched Max's wrist. "When we were at the celebration of life today, Patty's father mentioned trying for a baby with IVF. His wife left after the switch, so he'll be a single parent. But we're a couple, so we wouldn't have to worry about medical intervention or parenting alone."

Max swiveled forward and shook their hand away from Jo's grasp. "I don't want a baby." They couldn't imagine taking care of another life when they couldn't even manage their own.

Jo pouted.

The server returned to gather their empty salad plates.

The air crackled with static, and Max felt something shift.

I should have kept my mouth shut.

Max widened their eyes. They could hear Jo's thoughts as clearly as if she had spoken the words aloud.

But if I keep my needs to myself, they will never get met. Jo rapidly blinked her eyes.

Max knew she was trying to prevent a crying jag from ruining her makeup.

With a napkin, Jo dabbed at the corners of her eyes.

The server returned with their entrées.

"You know, I didn't want children at first," Candy said. "I bet you didn't either when you were a man."

Jo sniffed, then nodded. "You're right, Candy. I didn't. My wife did."

"So, don't be hard on Max, please. They'll come around."

Max stiffened in the chair. With their foot, they nudged Candy's shin under the table. They didn't think they would "come around" to wanting children. So, why had Candy said it?

"Stop that," Candy said, narrowing her gaze. "I'm speaking the truth with love."

"You know I've always wanted children," Eli said while cutting into his steak. "But when I mention it on dates, the women always freak out."

"On what date do you mention it?" Candy asked, twirling a fork in her linguine.

"The first." A deep blush covered Eli's face.

"That's your problem." Candy wagged a finger at him. "Wait until you've been seeing each other for a couple of months. My wife didn't tell me she wanted kids until after we married, which I feel is too late. A guy needs some time to consider it before making the commitment, not the other way around."

Max stared at the calamari steak for a long moment, hoping to transmit their thoughts. *Jo, I'm sorry for upsetting you. I just don't want to bring another human being into this mixed-up world.*

With a forkful of lobster in her mouth, Jo widened her eyes. *Things are getting better now that everyone's transitioned.*

Max speared a piece of asparagus with their fork. *Everyone? Only certain people are affected. If we have a boy, we won't have to worry until he hits his fifties. But if we have a girl, we might live to see her become an old man like me.* They glowered at Jo across the table and shoved the asparagus into their mouth.

Jo looked defeated. The thoughts had pummeled her from the inside out. She hunched her shoulders, curling into a tight ball.

Eli touched her elbow. "Are you all right?"

How dare he? Max let the fork clatter to the table. "She's fine."

"She doesn't look fine." Eli spun toward Max. "She looks sick to her stomach, like something—or should I say, someone—isn't agreeing with her."

Max fumed. "So, you can hear my thoughts too." They scooted back in the chair until it almost tipped over. "Respect our privacy. Or leave. I never wanted you here anyway. It was Jo's idea. I only wanted Candy to come."

At the mention of her name, Candy's eyes widened. "What's happening?" She craned her neck to glance up at Max, who stood, towering above the others at the table. "I don't understand what's going on."

Stunned, Max pointed from Eli to Jo. "These two created a software program that runs on your brain, translating thoughts into messages you can send to others. But the program is flawed, and everyone who had the software installed can hear anyone's thoughts at any time as long as the person thinking had the software installed at one time."

Candy gaped. "Are you saying you guys are having a conversation with your thoughts?"

Nodding, Max gnarled his hands into fists. "I was thinking with Jo until Eli butted in."

Jo stood, waving for everyone to sit down. "Let's be civil and finish dinner with an out-loud conversation, shall we?"

As soon as Max returned to the plush seat, they felt all the anger and frustration pool in their limbs. A part of them still wanted to strike back at Jo, at Eli, at the world to defend the right to the privacy of their thoughts, the sacredness of their bodies, but the other part of them knew that fighting required too much effort. They didn't want to die trying like Patty had, but they didn't want to stride over to Jo and kiss her as a peace offering either. With a sigh of resignation, they decided to blank out their thoughts and focus on the calamari steak.

When the meal was finished, Jo paid the bill.

The server stopped by for the check and handed Max a slice of chocolate cake.

Jo, Eli, and Candy sang "Happy Birthday."

Max stared at the single candle and made a wish—to

be a young woman again. They didn't care if Jo and Eli heard their thoughts. They wanted it more than anything in the world. Ever since becoming an old man, their soul had been straining against the seams of their aging body that required more and more effort just to get through each day. Therapy helped, not the individual therapy with the daily mantras and affirmations, but the group kind, where the people talked about their experiences of living in a peculiar body and how that new body affected everything—from going to the bathroom to having sex.

"Would anyone like a bite?" Max asked, passing the plate around the table.

Candy waved away the cake, citing her need to watch her figure.

"It's only one bite," Jo said, eyeing Candy's body. "You'll burn off the calories from just breathing."

"No, thanks," she said, removing her phone from her purse. "I need to text Sarah and see how long it will take for her to come pick me up."

"I can drive you home," Eli offered.

"Really?" Candy asked.

"Of course. I'd love to." Eli widened his smile.

"Okay." Candy shrugged and shoved her phone back into her purse. "At least I know I'll get home safely." She wagged her finger at Eli. "Unless you drive as crazy as Sarah does."

"Crazier." He winked.

Candy giggled.

Max had never heard Candy make that tittering sound. They cocked their head to the side and glanced from Candy to Eli and back again.

"Shall we?" Jo stood and gathered her purse. She held out her arm, and Max shuffled around the table to link their arm through hers. She patted their hand. "I'm sorry for mentioning the baby."

Max rubbed her knuckles. "Let's not talk about it right now, okay?"

"Okay."

Instead of going through the restaurant to the front entrance, Max wove their way through the tables to the side exit to the parking lot. As they left the heat lamps and the warm ambiance, the bite of night air sent a chill running up their legs, and their joints stiffened. Behind them, Eli's deep voice and Candy's high-pitched chuckle punctuated the darkening night like audible stars.

"I think they like each other," Jo said.

Max agreed, "They do."

In the parking lot, Max released Jo's arm and hugged Candy, promising to call and get together on her day off.

"Nice meeting you, Jo." Candy waved before sliding into Eli's car.

"Likewise," Jo said. But the muscle twitching in her cheek said otherwise.

Max watched Eli's car weave through the parking lot before braking at the exit. While waiting for traffic to pass, the car idled beneath a streetlight. The yellow glow illuminated the inside of the cab, where Eli and Candy sat with their heads tipped close to each other. A flare of heat spread across Max's chest.

They grabbed Jo's hand and squeezed her fingers. "Are you jealous?"

"Hardly," Jo said, unlocking the doors of her sports car. She glanced at Max and smiled. "I have you, don't I?"

"I'm not as funny as Eli or as generous as Candy or as smart as you," Max said.

"But you're you," Jo said, bending to kiss their lips.

The brush of her mouth sent a shiver of pleasure throughout Max's body. "I'm sorry for being upset when you said you wanted a baby." The apology was sincere, and a softness entered their body, releasing all the pent-up pain that had accumulated over the weeks.

"Apology accepted."

Max settled into the passenger seat and waited while Jo fiddled with the controls, turning up the heat. "I know you've done everything to make me better, and I appreciate it." They rubbed their hands together before the vents and let the warmth thaw the chill from their joints. "I especially enjoyed tonight's birthday dinner."

"Did you?" Jo asked, backing up the vehicle.

"Well, not our fight or Eli's card, but just knowing everyone was there because of me made me feel less alone and useless."

"You're not alone, and you're definitely not useless."

"I feel that way at work, shadowing you." Max gulped. "I thought I'd like working in business, but it's not what I expected."

"Do you want to do something else?"

Max leaned against the door, gazing out the window at the buildings lit from within, like giant birthday candles, one after another. They thought about the time they had left, not knowing if it would be days or weeks or months or years, and how they would like to spend it. "I'd like to learn how to cook. I want to have dinner ready for you when you come home." They thought some more. "And I'd like to spend more time with Candy. She keeps me grounded. I like having a friend who's been my age."

"So, does that mean you're putting in your two-week notice?" Jo kept her gaze on the road as she turned down their street and slowed to go over the speed bumps.

"Yes." Max meant it. They wanted to see what the remaining days had to offer, even if they weren't what they expected.

"And what about a baby?" Jo asked, driving the car into the garage. She turned off the engine and closed the garage door and sat in silence, waiting.

Max propped open their door, and the cab filled with light. They stared at Jo. She was so young, so hopeful, so full of life. Of course she wanted a child. They glanced away, at the floorboards and their feet. Everyone should consider the moral implications of bringing new life into the world. When she had been Maxine, she wouldn't have pondered the question, wouldn't have thought about getting pregnant, wouldn't have considered anything beyond her immediate concerns of moving out, starting a career, and becoming independent. But now, in the darkness of their condition and the urgency of Jo's desire, they were forced to confront their worst fears.

"Who will help you raise a child if I'm not around?"

Without hesitation, Jo said, "Your mother."

"My mother?" Max glanced up and gaped.

Jo shrugged. "Why not?"

"She doesn't talk to me, and she hates you. Why would she help you raise our child?"

"Because that's what grandmothers do." Jo slipped out of the car. She circled around the bumper and stopped beside Max's open door. "Are you coming inside?"

Dumbfounded into silence, Max stared at her for a long moment before they took her hand and followed her up the stairs and into the house.

CHAPTER 21

On Monday morning, Max hobbled into the lab, where Dr. Dio bent over a strand of what looked like oversize ticker tape.

Max knocked on the doorjamb. "Do you have a minute?"

Without glancing up from the endless strip of paper, Dr. Dio said, "Have a seat."

Max glanced at the uncomfortable-looking chair against the wall and chose to stand. They crossed their arms over their chest and waited. The lab wasn't as sophisticated as Max had imagined. It looked more like a converted office space with medical equipment—from an examination chair to an electroencephalogram machine. Max didn't know the size and scope of the previous lab, so they had no idea whether these accommodations were sufficient for whatever Dr. Dio needed to do to convert thoughts into usable energy.

After winding the paper like a huge ribbon, Dr. Dio set it on the counter and patted it with his small hand. "Neurological impulses," he explained. When he smiled, his small eyes slanted behind large black glasses. He was a short man, but a few inches taller than Max. "How can I help you today?"

"You mean, you can't hear my thoughts?" Max smirked, assuming everyone who had worked on the brain-to-brain project had the software installed at one time or another.

"No. Should I?" Dr. Dio furrowed his brow.

"Jo and Eli can." Max tapped their foot against the linoleum floor. The sound echoed louder than it should. They breathed in deeply. The whole room smelled sterile.

"Sit." Dr. Dio waved to the chair. "You make me nervous, standing."

Max complied, hiking up their slacks and sinking into the plastic seat.

Dr. Dio sat on an examination stool. He swiveled over to Max and clasped his hands between his knees. The white lab coat closed over his blue suit. "Start at the beginning so I have all the facts, please."

With a sharp intake of breath, Max told Dr. Dio everything—from the software installation to hearing Patty's and their father's voices to discovering that Jo and Eli could hear their thoughts. "Not all the time," they said, "but enough to be disturbing." They rubbed their palms against their thighs and swallowed. "I have no privacy. I'm scared to think anymore."

Dr. Dio listened without comment. He rubbed his chin thoughtfully, his eyes squinting, his brow even more deeply furrowed. "I understand your concern. That's why the FCC banned the project and fined the company. Thank goodness no one can sue because of the nondisclosure and hold-harmless agreements." He shook his head. "I wish I could do something to stop the intrusion, but I can't." He removed his glasses and rubbed his eyes. "I tried. Trust me, I did everything in my power. But I can't get rid of the entire software program without eliminating vital neurological functions." He slipped the glasses up the bridge of his nose. "I'm sorry."

A spike of panic seized Max's chest, and they felt their breath quicken. "So, there's no cure for this unwanted and unpredictable telepathy?"

"No," Dr. Dio said. "And if you still have the software installed, it's probably embedded itself throughout your cerebrum. I can't uninstall it without erasing your memory or damaging the corpus callosum, which connects the two hemispheres of your brain."

"What does that mean?" Max shifted against the hard seat. An uneasy prickle tingled in their feet.

Dr. Dio swiveled over to a laptop propped on a movable table next to the examination chair. He tapped on the keyboard and brought up an image of the human brain. With his index finger, he pointed. "The software is installed here, and once it's installed, it sends impulses here and here." His finger traced the pathways, like tiny roads moving around the brain and ending up at the beginning like a huge, tangled mess. "Because of this patterning, the software becomes a permanent part of you." He dropped his hand into his lap and faced Max. "You will always be able to communicate telepathically with whoever once had the software installed, even after its removal. Because those who had the program uninstalled only have trace amounts embedded in their neural pathways, the communication will always be sporadic and unreliable." He lifted his hands, palms up, like he was surrendering. "Some experiments just fail."

The numbness flowed up Max's legs. "Nothing is sacred with you guys, is it?"

All those collegiate lessons they had learned about business had been useless. Perfect theories in an imperfect world. The reality was, commerce always tipped in favor of innovation, of creating a demand for the supply of someone's manipulative invention. The truth was, every problem a business solved created another larger problem to be tackled further down the line. Need more efficient transportation and energy? Get the fossil fuel crisis. Want lighter, more affordable containers for shipping and storage? Get the plastic crisis. Need to communicate immediately, no devices needed? Get the thought crisis.

In the hollow of a breast pocket, Max's phone pinged.

"Excuse me." Max fished out the phone and swiped a finger across the screen.

—*I hope you remembered your father's death day. I already placed flowers on his grave.*—

Max hunched their shoulders and gritted their teeth. The value of a beloved's lost life was more important than the value of the beloved who remained. Max grunted as they thrust the phone back into their pocket. Sometimes, they wished they had never been born.

"Are you okay?" Dr. Dio asked.

Max's lower lip trembled. "It's my mother. She forgot my birthday yesterday, but she remembered my father had died today."

"I'm sorry." Dr. Dio shook his head. "You've had a bad run, haven't you?"

Max smirked. "More like a whirlwind of events out of my control."

"Control is an illusion," Dr. Dio said, standing. He strode over to the counter and placed his hand on the stack of papers charting neurological impulses. "We always think our choices determine our destiny, but often, it is the events in which we have no say that form our lives."

"Like my body and my thoughts?" Max grabbed the arms of the chair. With one strained movement, they rocked to their feet. The numbness had left their legs, leaving only a trace of pinpricks.

"You are not your body or your thoughts," Dr. Dio said. "Your body is just a case, and your thoughts are just impulses. The core of who you are is something science cannot measure."

Max paused in the doorway. "Then what am I?"

Dr. Dio lifted his palms. "Science has no answer."

"Thanks, Doc." Max sneered, turning into the hallway.

An urgency to lash out at someone responsible for this unprecedented circumstance flooded their system. They marched down the hallway. All their energy balled up into a fierce heat in their chest.

I need to confront Jo.

"Max, stop! She's meeting with an investor." Eli's voice, sharp and crisp, sliced through the static in their mind.

Glancing over their shoulder, they saw him racing down the hallway. His tie flew over his shoulder. His curly hair bounced across his forehead. His mouth parted, though no words escaped. Had the whole exchange happened between their minds, or had it been spoken aloud? Max couldn't tell anymore. But however it'd happened, it was enough to make them halt three strides away from Jo's closed office door.

"You called me by my name," Max said.

"I didn't know you preferred it over Maxi until I heard you think it yesterday." A sheepish expression traveled over Eli's face. "I'm sorry. I wish I had known sooner." The naked admission and genuine apology splashed across his face.

Max couldn't help but feel a ripple of pleasure. Maybe there was a benefit to others having access to one's thoughts. The raw honesty was something that couldn't be faked or denied. It stripped away all pretenses and excuses, destroyed all artificial barriers meant to segregate and protect, and invited a unity that otherwise couldn't exist.

"I should have said something earlier."

"Why didn't you?" Eli stopped a foot away.

Max shrugged. "It was easier to say nothing and believe you were a jerk."

Eli laughed. "I'm not a jerk. Just a nerd. There's a difference." He touched Max's elbow, guiding them away from the closed door. "Is there something I can help you with while Jo's in her meeting?"

Max glanced from Eli's hand on their arm to his warm, welcoming face. The anger and frustration they had felt over the failed thought experiment and the current thought-to-energy conversion process suddenly fell away, leaving a nothingness that stretched endlessly before them. What did it matter? Someone would always be inventing something in the perpetual wheel of scientific evolution. Why not Jo? Who was Max to stop her from exploiting the possibilities? At least, with their guidance and suggestions, maybe the process would be kinder, gentler, and more humane than it would be with someone else.

"No, there isn't," Max said.

"But you looked so purposeful." Eli frowned. "You even said you wanted to confront her."

"I did, but I changed my mind."

"Why?"

Max heaved a sigh. They had known both Joe and Jo, and although the differences were apparent—Joe with his stylish suits and bottom-line mentality and Jo with her endless accessories and concern for how her actions impacted others—the core remained the same. Both would always be ambitious, seeking to pioneer something somehow, someway, regardless of whether it succeeded or failed or how the effects would ripple out throughout the world. It was their nature, and Max was no longer naive enough to believe they were powerful enough to change someone's nature.

"Sometimes, you just need to let things be."

Eli nodded, matching Max's slow stride. At the doorway to Max's office, he stopped. "Jo mentioned you were quitting. Is it because of me?"

There was no point in lying if Eli could hear their thoughts. "I can't stand around, watching you fall in love with my woman." They grimaced. "I'm an old man. I can't beat you up in the back room. And I know enough about business to not ask her to fire you. You're a team, and you were a team long before I came into the picture." They shrugged. "So, it's best if I leave."

"Don't leave." An urgency flooded his voice. "Yes, I was falling for Jo, but only because she's an attractive woman. When she was a man, I didn't have any interest." A deep flush colored his face.

The admission defused the heat in Max's chest. The validation was good, but the victory was short-lived. "I can't stand around, watching you two flirt with each other."

Eli lifted his shoulders. "It's different now that I've met Candy." A dreamy look entered his eyes, and a soft smile played on his lips. "We connect on so many levels.

I need to thank you for bringing her yesterday. She's everything I've always imagined in the perfect woman for me."

"Perfect woman?" Max sneered. "Candy was an old man just months ago."

"But she's a young woman now," Eli said, broadening his stance. "And I think she's falling for me."

Max bit back a bitter response. They knew Eli was speaking the truth because they could hear his thoughts reminiscing over Candy's early morning text to him, saying how excited she was to have met such a gentleman with a good sense of humor and asking when she would see him again. The stark honesty sent a shock wave of disbelief throughout their old body.

Was Candy's intrusion into the love triangle, making it a rather odd square, a temporary distraction or a permanent solution? Max didn't know. Whatever happened between Candy and Eli would only take place outside of working hours. The rest of the time, Eli would be with Jo, developing something with the same intensity and devotion others spent creating a family, which was what Jo wanted after all and the one thing she had asked of Max. A child.

But Max knew from watching families all around him fall apart that a child was the last thing to bring a couple together. Right now, Jo was bound to them through love, history, and a shared residence. Was it enough? Max didn't know, and the uncertainty troubled them.

"I can't stay," Max said. "I wish you and Candy all the best, but I have some things I'd like to do with whatever time I have left in this world."

Eli waved a hand up and down the length of Max's body. "You're in great shape. Why talk as if you're dying?"

Although Max was young and inexperienced and naive inside their old-man body, they knew Jo's financial stability allowed for the fulfillment of their original plan —financial independence, retire early—which made the rest of their life easy to manage.

"I appreciate the compliment, Eli, but I've made other plans."

CHAPTER 22

As soon as Max quit, they formed a new routine to structure their days. Every morning, they made breakfast for Jo. Omelets, pancakes, French toast, waffles, or smoothies. Once Jo left for work, they tended to the garden, watering and fertilizing, pruning and weeding. Next, they attended a restorative yoga class at the senior center. After lunch, they watched a show on the Food Network for cooking ideas and shopped for any ingredients needed to make dinner. By the time Jo arrived home, they had dinner in the oven and the table set. Although the routine was simple, repetitive, and easy to follow, each day was fuller and more satisfying than the last.

One evening, Jo sat at the dining room table, reading the news on her phone and summarizing the highlights for Max. Almost everybody in politics had switched, except for a handful of people who were unaffected. The president, once an old man, had become a young woman —too young to govern by the current rules. Congress struggled with whether to invoke the twenty-fifth amendment or pass another one, lowering the age from thirty-five to twenty-one. Those in favor of replacing the president cited section four, but those against it stated it didn't cover this contingency.

"I think they should just amend the Constitution," Jo said. "What about you?"

Max shrugged. They were finishing up a recipe they'd discovered while watching a program on the Food Network. "I've always thought skill and experience were more valuable than age."

Nodding, Jo resumed reading.

Another issue had been raised, as a third of the Senate and the House of Representatives had suddenly become pregnant. Most of the constituents hailed from states where birth control and abortion had been banned, so they faced the prospects of carrying these unwanted pregnancies to term. During the day, sometimes, Max flipped through the channels, catching snippets from commentators who worried who would fill the vacancies during parental leave, how many of the new mothers would finish their terms, and how many would elect to stay home and parent. The talk shows were full of controversies over the options presented, and the public started to become restless. Max wondered if the streets would be filled with protests again.

"Don't worry," Jo said, flipping her phone face down on the table. "Most of those states are hustling to put abortion back into place. I don't think we'll see the protests we saw in the spring when people first started switching ages and genders."

Max set a glass of water and a plate of chicken Parmesan with spaghetti and creamed spinach on the table.

"Thanks, hon," Jo said without glancing up. "Do you think we're on our way to becoming a matriarchy?"

Max took the seat next to her and cut into their chicken Parmesan. "I don't think we're there yet. Too many people are in that liminal space, not sure of who they are or what they think anymore."

The chicken Parmesan was perfect inside and tasted tender, not chewy, like the chicken Marsala they had made last week. But the creamed spinach had a touch too much salt. They gulped a mouthful of lukewarm soda and winced at the temperature. They had arrived home late, after spending too much time dodging through the grocery store to avoid their mother, who they'd recognized in the produce section, examining the butternut squash. In their haste to prepare dinner, they had forgotten their opened can of soda on the counter while they cooked. They stood and strode over to the sink and dumped out the fizzy brown fluid and popped the can on a new soda from the fridge. Their phone buzzed on the counter, and they swiped a finger across the screen. It was a text from Candy.

—*We had another employee quit. Do you want a job at The Spirit Store? I'm hiring.*—

Just a year ago, Max had imagined working for a company in accounting or human resources or project management. But the stint at Jo's company had proven they weren't cut out for business. They preferred spending their days either cooking in the kitchen, puttering around in the garden, or taking long walks with Jo.

They pocketed the phone and slurped their soda. "Candy wants to know if I'd like a job at The Spirit Store."

Frowning, Jo straightened her spine and set her fork against her plate. "I thought you didn't like working." She dabbed her mouth with a napkin and waited.

The opportunity to spend time with Candy and earn a few dollars, if only part-time and temporary, appealed to them.

Max sank into the chair next to Jo. "I never said I didn't like working. I said I didn't like shadowing you."

"And how would working for Candy be any different?" Jo crumpled the napkin in her fist. "You'll be surrounded by teenagers and young adults floating through life. Do you think that's a healthy environment?"

Max glanced down at the age spots speckling their hands. They understood Jo's concerns, but they didn't agree with her. The temptations of youth didn't appeal to them. They had thought stretching with other elderly people who couldn't reach their toes would give them a sense of belonging, but that class only increased their feeling of alienation, stranded in a nebulous world in which they didn't belong. Staying home wasn't an option. They might end up like their mother, addicted to daytime TV and conspiracy theories. Being with Candy would be different. Candy understood them. If Candy was managing The Spirit Store, then that was where Max wanted to be.

"Don't worry about the environment. If it's unhealthy, I'll quit. Just like I quit working with you." Their voice sounded solid, like steel.

Jo lifted her eyebrows and released the balled-up napkin on the table. She grasped Max's hand. "Okay. But don't overdo it. I like having you here, cooking for me. I don't want you worn out and tired all the time."

"Don't worry," Max said, squeezing her hand. "I'll take it easy, I promise."

CHAPTER 23

Working in retail was a lot like working at home. Pick up, clean up, put away. Over and over again.

The store was huge. A maze had been set up in the middle of the shop floor, like one of those corn mazes in pumpkin patches. The children would run through the narrow halls and scream and yell and sometimes fall and scrape their knees on the linoleum floor. Max and the others—Candy, her granddaughter, and two of her granddaughters' friends—took turns between reshelving costumes and ringing up purchases.

Max didn't mind the ghoulish chatter from the automated decorations or the dry ice clouds floating from the fake witch's brew, but they did mind the constant bending and squatting to pick up costumes that had fallen from the racks. Even with their daily walks and yoga exercises, they struggled to maintain balance.

"Watch out, Pops," Dan said.

Max ducked just before the moving drawbridge lowered. The castle had been erected over the weekend to entice customers to buy it, and the display was more dangerous than the maze and more annoying than the remote-controlled flying bats.

"Go to the register," Candy said. She grabbed the glittering wings and sparkling tiaras out of their hands. "I've got this."

"Thanks." Max watched her graceful form bend and stretch as she restocked the items.

A ball of envy lodged in the pit of their stomach. They used to be more catlike—lithe and agile with nine lives for accidents. Now they were more cattle-like—slow and plodding and easily tipped over. While their coworkers strode confidently through the aisles, they shuffled carefully in black orthopedic shoes. During their ten-minute breaks, their coworkers stepped outside to vape and chat while they sat with their legs propped on a vinyl chair to ease the pain in their joints. More than once, they feared Jo was right. Working retail wasn't a healthy environment for them—not because of their youthful coworkers, but because of the physical demands.

Max hobbled around the cash area and stood, waiting for customers. They only worked weekday mornings and early afternoons because they wanted to be home before Jo so they could cook dinner. Despite sighting their mother once, they liked stopping at the grocery store, gathering any items needed for the meal they would prepare each night—brown sugar pork chops with wild rice and baby carrots, or fresh salmon with red potatoes and asparagus. Since the first sighting, they had noticed their mother twice at the other end of the produce section, squeezing tomatoes, testing for freshness. Both times, they'd avoided her, steering their cart abruptly down another aisle, their heartbeat thumping in their chest. They didn't want her to witness their unwilling transition from young to old, from female to male. They didn't want her judgment, but they needed to shop.

Cooking for Jo brought satisfaction and purpose, an exquisite work of edible art and a punctuation mark to end each day.

Max was thinking about the menu for tonight when they noticed a woman with a familiar side-to-side shuffle pushing a shopping cart full of Halloween decorations. Their stomach clenched.

Mom.

The jolt of recognition sent them into a panic, and they grabbed the intercom and asked for assistance. While they waited, their mouth dried up. They hoped she would stop to select a few last-minute items, but she barreled toward them like a bowling ball aiming for a strike.

In the distance, Dan waved his hand, signaling he would relieve them. Relief showered over Max, but the sensation was short-lived, as Dan was sidetracked by one customer after another.

A light sweat beaded across Max's forehead, and they removed a handkerchief from their breast pocket and mopped up the moisture.

By now, their mother had arrived at the cash area. One by one, she reached inside the cart and stacked the items on the counter. She worked methodically with her head bent and her arms swinging like rusted cranes.

Max swallowed, glancing from their mother to the castle, where Dan dodged children. *Hurry, hurry, hurry.* Max focused their thoughts, trying to transmit them to Dan, though they suspected the effort was pointless. Why would Dan have been one of the handful of volunteers of the brain-to-brain experiment?

Their mother plucked the final item out of her cart and wedged it against the others on the counter.

"Find everything okay?" Max asked, scanning a plastic jack-o'-lantern.

"Oh, I suppose I did," she said, hoisting her purse into the child's seat in the shopping cart. With her head still bent, she rummaged through the contents for her wallet. "Been lonely since my daughter moved out. Thought decorating for the neighborhood kids would be nice."

"Mmhmm," Max said, scanning a box of a blow-up spider for the lawn.

"I don't need a bag." She found her wallet and waved to the shopping cart. "I'll just wheel everything to my car."

Max glanced over her head across the castle and the maze, searching for his backup. Where was Dan? They could no longer spot him.

Their mother tapped her credit card against the payment terminal and waited until the screen said *Approved* before she slipped it back into her wallet. After she zipped up her purse, she lifted her gaze for a moment.

She leaned forward and squinted. "Do I know you?"

Max smelled her powdery scent—the same fragrance they had grown up with and adored. "I don't think so," they said, crossing their fingers behind their back to counteract the lie.

She deepened her frown, and her forehead creased. "You look like my dead husband."

Dan jogged up to the front of the store. "Sorry it took so long," he said, arriving behind the counter. "Ready for your break, Pops?"

Max didn't move or acknowledge him. Their heart was ticking in their chest, and their gaze was focused on their mom.

"Rupert, is that you?" she asked.

Max hadn't heard their father's name spoken in years.

With a gentle nudge, Dan said, "Log out, Pops. I'll finish with her."

"We're done," Max said, glancing away, hoping to break the spell.

But their mom had recognized them. "It's you. Oh my goodness, it's you."

Dan laughed, pointing to the silicone face masks in a nearby aisle. "His costume looks real, right?"

"It's a costume?" She tilted her head.

Max logged out of the register and took a step back.

Dan slid into position. With a smile, he handed her the receipt. "Do you need help out, ma'am?"

"Yes, thank you."

Max shuffled toward the nearest employee exit, feeling the heat of their mom's gaze against their back. Their joints creaked with guilt, shame, and betrayal. Dan had tried to save them. But they didn't think his efforts had amounted to much. Their mom might be temporarily confused, but she wasn't senile or stupid. She knew it was them.

After a stop in the gender-neutral restroom, they hobbled into the break room. The air was thick with the scent of chocolate doughnuts and stale coffee. They sank into a vinyl chair and put up their feet on another, letting the tension release from their muscles. Their cell phone vibrated in their breast pocket. After swiping a finger across the screen, they read the message.

—*That was you, wasn't it?*—

They gulped, staring at the message from their mom. The phone vibrated again.

—*Why didn't you tell me you'd switched?*—

A response played through their mind. *Why would I*

tell you? I don't need your judgment.

The words formed on the screen, and Max pressed the backspace key until the screen was blank. Clenching their jaw, they shoved the phone into their breast pocket. They had nothing to say to their mom. Nothing at all.

Upon their arrival home from work, Max entered the great room from the garage and bypassed the vacant kitchen. They unlaced their orthopedic shoes and tucked them into the cubby by the front door and shuffled to the primary bedroom and crawled into bed.

An hour or so later, they heard Jo call out, "Max, honey, where are you?"

They closed their eyes, pretending to sleep on top of the bedspread, their hands folded over their belly, the steady rise and fall of their chest lulling them into a state of calm.

Jo strode into the bedroom and perched at the edge of the mattress. Her cool fingers stroked Max's arm beneath the short shirtsleeve. "Honey," she whispered, "are you all right?"

Max blinked their eyes like a turtle. The world slowly shifted into focus. They gazed up at Jo's loving and caring face, the skin between her plucked eyebrows pinched into a tiny V.

They gulped. "I saw my mom at work today. She knows I switched."

"Did she harass you?" Jo frowned, and her fingers trailed down the length of their arm and laced with their fingers.

With their other arm, Max retrieved their cell phone from the nightstand. "Look."

Jo released Max's hand, grabbed the phone, and swiped the screen. After scrolling through the messages, she frowned. "Will you text her back?"

"Why should I?" Max snatched the phone out of Jo's hand and folded their arms over their chest.

"She's your mom. She's concerned."

"She thought I was my father. She called me Rupert in the store."

How could Max explain the situation to Jo? Neither of her parents was alive. She didn't have to contend with family gatherings or misunderstandings or unspoken expectations. She was free. Max wasn't.

Jo stroked Max's forehead and planted a kiss on their crown. "Is that why you're upset?"

Hardness steeled their back. They set the phone face down on the nightstand. "I don't know."

She touched their hand again. "I think you should call and invite her over for dinner. She must be lonely without you."

"I don't want anything to do with her," Max said, tugging their hand free and rolling onto their side. With their back to Jo, they shoved their fists beneath the pillow. "She hates me. And I hate her."

"*Hate* is a strong word," Jo said, stroking their back. "Why don't you let bygones be bygones before it's too late?"

Too late. The phrase lodged in Max's mind. "Neither one of us is dying."

"Anyone can die at any time for any reason," Jo said. "You don't have to be dying to make amends."

But all Max could hear was the derision in their mom's voice and the disdain in her texted questions. They had never been good enough as a young woman, and now, with their father's face, they would not be good enough again. They felt something tighten in their chest, and they rubbed the sore spot with a fist, worried it might be something more than just tension, that it might be the first signs of heart disease—because they didn't believe anyone could truly die from a broken heart.

CHAPTER 24

The next day, Max sat with their feet propped on a vinyl chair in the break room of The Spirit Store. They sipped from a glass of water on the table.

"Hey, you." Candy's granddaughter, Sarah, flounced into the room, smelling like lavender essential oil.

She had shaved half her blonde hair and dyed the rest flamingo pink and pierced a steel bar through her nostrils. Max didn't find the look professional or attractive, but no one cared what they thought. They were old, out of it, and no longer in touch with what was trending.

Sarah shoved a hand into the pocket of her baggy pants and withdrew a handful of gummy bears. "Have you tried taking CBD for your arthritis?" She placed the colorful bears on the table by the glass of water.

Max blinked. They pinched a sticky green-colored gummy bear between two fingers.

Candy strolled into the room and swooped between them. "Don't be giving those to them. You don't know how they'll interact with any medications they're on." She plucked the gummy bear from Max's fingers and pocketed the rest in her jeans. "Go back to work and leave Max alone."

Sarah narrowed her gaze, but did as she had been told. The scent of lavender exited the room.

"Sheesh." Candy poured a cup of black coffee, grabbed a sandwich from the refrigerator, flopped onto a chair across from Max, and shook her head. "I hate having to discipline her, but her mother lets her get away with murder."

Max shrugged. "She cares. That's more than I can say about most people."

"She's young and dumb." She unwrapped the sandwich, the same one she had every day—ham and cheese with a thin smear of mayonnaise. She dunked it into the black coffee and took a bite.

Max shuddered. They could never get used to Candy's old-man habits. As much as Candy tried, she would never fit in with the youngsters with their designer coffee, healthy wraps, and alternative medicine.

"I'm not on any prescription drugs. I could use a gummy. My feet are killing me today."

Candy glanced at the clock against the wall. "Shouldn't you be heading back? It's been ten and then some."

"Don't get started on me, sister," Max said. "I'm not your granddaughter. You can't boss me around."

"But I can fire you." She snickered, dunking her sandwich into the coffee.

"Go ahead." Max slid their legs off the chair and stood. "Who else will you hire with only a couple of weeks left till Halloween?"

"Ha-ha, very funny," Candy said. "That's what temp agencies are for."

Max couldn't win. They didn't have enough experience to fire back a response. They took two steps toward the exit and paused. Their thoughts drifted toward their mom, Jo's comments about reconciliation, and how long they might have to live, even though they didn't have any health problems.

"May I ask you something?"

"Make it quick. Your break's over." Candy set aside her sandwich and folded her arms on the table.

"My mom came by the other day and recognized me. She sent a couple of texts, and they weren't nice. I haven't responded, but Jo thinks I should. Would you?"

Candy twisted her lips. "Depends. Moms have a way of making grown men feel like little boys again. Do you love her?"

Love. The word felt foreign even though Max knew what the word meant and how it felt when they were with Jo.

"It's complicated."

"Then wait. Wait until you feel so guilty that you have to respond. That's what I did. And I have no regrets. I didn't talk to my mom for five years because she had kept nagging my wife for a grandbaby. We tried. But it took five years until it happened. When she finally realized it wasn't our fault—that we hadn't been purposefully withholding a grandbaby from her—she finally eased up on the guilt trip."

Max nodded. Did they or their mom have five years left, and would a baby fix the fissure in their relationship?

"Anything else?" Candy eyed them. "There's something else—I know it. You get that look on your face —all sheepish—and then you turn away. Say it."

A brief chuckle escaped from their lips, and they smiled. It felt good to be seen by someone who cared. "I'm worried Jo might leave me for someone who can give her the family she wants."

"Doesn't matter what she wants." Candy pointed to Max's chest. "What do you want?"

A blank expanse of nothingness unfolded before them. They hadn't considered what they wanted in terms of their relationship.

"I don't know."

Candy heaved a sigh. "You need to figure it out. Don't let anyone pressure you." She wagged a finger at them. "I know you're a man, but you were once a woman, and women tend to let the guys take charge. You're in charge now. Don't let Jo's desires back you into a corner. Decide what you want and then go for it."

"Is that what you're doing with Eli?"

Max hadn't asked Candy for specifics about her budding relationship with Eli, but they wanted to know how to do things right. Candy had been married for over fifty years, and she had more experience than anyone Max knew in terms of intimate relationships.

A soft wistfulness fluttered across Candy's face, and she smiled. "He helps me feel like a woman." She waved a hand at her clothes. "Sure, I dress the part, but Eli makes me feel like it's okay to be a woman with all those crazy hormones and emotions." She tilted her head to the side. "It's good, not being a man anymore. I don't have to make all the decisions. I can let Eli pick out where to go and what to eat. And I always let him pay." She winked. "It's liberating, you know?"

Max didn't know. When she had been a woman, she'd always felt trapped by the circumstance of living with her mother. Now that they had a different body, they no longer felt like a woman, but they also didn't feel like a man. They still let Jo make most of the decisions, and they still felt a little crazy at times even though they could no longer blame estrogen for the problem. This nebulous state left them confused. No one seemed to have an answer.

"Jo likes being a woman. She said she likes it better than when she was a man."

"I agree," Candy said. "Now get back to work."

With a brief nod, Max turned and shuffled out of the break room.

As they rang up customer after customer, they searched the faces of toddlers and preschoolers who clutched their costumes to their chests, their toothy smiles full of delight and wonder at the magic of the season. A softness started to work around the edges of their mind, and by the time they clocked out and headed to the parking lot in the drizzly rain, they knew what they needed to do.

CHAPTER 25

A t home, Max prepared an elaborate dinner—filet mignon with a rich balsamic glaze, roasted red potatoes, green beans, and champagne. They had just dimmed the lights in the dining room when the garage door opened, and Jo clumped up the stairs into the kitchen.

She glanced at the set table, and her purse strap slipped down her arm and thumped on the hardwood floor. "Oh my goodness." Her hand covered her mouth, and tears glittered in her blue eyes. "What are we celebrating?"

Without answering, Max poured two glasses of champagne and offered one to her. "I know I've been a thorn in your side since I switched," they said, "but I want to thank you for sticking by me and helping me with everything. I wouldn't be here without you."

Jo set the champagne flute on the dining room table and covered her face with both hands.

"What's wrong?" The flute clattered against the edge of a plate when Max set it down. They stepped closer and wrapped their arms around Jo's back, pressing her trembling body against their solid one.

After Jo cried, she wriggled out of their arms and sniffed. "I'm scared."

"Why?" Confusion rocketed through Max's body.

They concentrated, trying to hear Jo's thoughts, but her mind was a brick wall.

"I heard voices today at work." She exhaled forcefully, pushing the air between her lips. "I went to see Dr. Dio, and he said there is nothing he can do."

"What type of voices?" Max asked. "Other people or from the other side?"

Jo threw up her arms. "I don't know." She scraped the legs of a dining room chair across the hardwood floor and sank into it. "I'm not feeling well. Between the fundraising efforts and the need for more staff, I'm so stressed that I've missed another period." She rubbed her forehead. "I'm thinking of skipping dinner and calling it a night."

For a long moment, Max stood still. "Have you taken a pregnancy test?"

Jo waved her hand. "I did last month, and it was negative. Why should I take one again?"

"To be sure it's just stress and not something else."

"Fine, I'll take one tomorrow."

Max glanced at the elaborate spread on the table, then at Jo's bowed head. They didn't know if the timing was wrong, but they felt an urgency they hadn't felt before, as if time was running out. Grabbing the edge of the table, they knelt before Jo. After taking a deep breath, they gathered the courage to say what they had rehearsed while preparing dinner. "Jo, you are the love of my life. Will you marry me?"

Jo dropped her hands into her lap and gaped. The candlelight flickered in her pupils like twin flames.

The silence stretched between them. Max's knees ached against the hardwood floor. "I can't stay here much longer." They didn't have a ring or a date. They only had love in their heart for Jo. "Will you be my wife?"

"Why now?" She closed her mouth and narrowed her gaze. "I thought you didn't want to get married, didn't want to have children, were content with what we have."

"I was."

"Then what happened?"

Max thought of the children they had seen at the checkout line. How happy and carefree they were. How haggard and pleasantly thrilled their parents had seemed to be.

They squeezed Jo's hand. "I can't be selfish anymore. It's not about me. It's about us. We're committed to each other. Why not make it official?"

Shaking her head, she grabbed a napkin from the table and dabbed under her eyes. "You sound so resolute. Like if we don't marry now, we'll never marry, and it will be my fault for not saying yes."

That wasn't the answer they had expected. Their shoulders sagged, and a sharp pain shot up their thighs. They sank on their haunches, burying their head in Jo's lap. Their body stiffened from disbelief.

They'd thought she would be overjoyed, throwing her arms around their neck and screaming, *Yes!*

What had gone wrong? And could they fix it?

"I love you," Jo said, stroking the back of their head with her fingertips. "I just don't want to get married and have a family anymore." She nudged Max's head from her lap and grabbed their hands, standing with them. She pointed to her flat stomach. "You were right the other night about being too old. If we have a baby now, you'll be almost one hundred by the time the child graduates from high school. How selfish is that?"

The words sounded familiar. The sentiments too.

But Max had resolved to give Jo her heart's desire.

And now Jo had changed her mind.

Which left Max dazed and confused.

Jo pressed a kiss against their lips. "Thanks for cooking, but I'm calling it a night."

Max watched her leave, taking their heart with her.

After a lackluster dinner alone, Max lay next to Jo, who curled up with her back to them. Her body rose and fell with each breath. Max wondered if she was sleeping or just pretending to be asleep. They didn't want to shake her shoulder to find out. She was tired. They could talk tomorrow. But would talking do any good?

As the minutes spun into hours, Max stared at the ceiling. It was just past midnight when they reached for their phone from the nightstand. After swiping the screen, they scrolled through their messages, finding the saved conversation thread with their mother. The unanswered question from a while back glowed.

—*Why didn't you tell me you'd switched?*—

For a long moment, Max hovered a finger above the keyboard before typing, no longer trusting the privacy of their thoughts.

—*I didn't want your judgment.*—

After sending the message, Max placed the phone face down on their chest. A few seconds later, the phone vibrated.

—*Judgment? It's not your fault you fell victim to the switch.*—

Max glanced at Jo's sleeping back. The burning in their gut felt like a betrayal. Without thinking, they typed.

—I want to come home.—

The seconds lapsed.

Max started counting. *One, two, three.*

By the time they reached one hundred twenty, their cell phone quivered.

—Why?—

Max stared at the question. A growing panic pounded in their chest. What could they say? *That love doesn't conquer all. That just because you change your mind, it doesn't mean the other person won't change their mind also.* All of it and none of it encapsulated what Max had learned.

Their heartbeat quickened into a drumbeat, and an uneasiness vibrated throughout their body. They wanted to escape to the comfort and familiarity of their old bedroom on the second floor of their mother's house. They wanted to lie in the snug twin bed and gaze through the window at the bare branches of the trees in the backyard.

Oh, how they missed the sky full of stars.

They flipped the phone over in their hands and typed.

—You were right. I need to be with someone my own age. —

This time, the response came more quickly.

—Move to a retirement home. I'm almost twenty years younger than you are now.—

—That's not what I meant.—

—Then what did you mean?—

—I can't do this anymore.—

—None of us can.—

The finality of the statement felt like a door slamming in their face. The fantasy of their childhood bedroom disappeared. Memories resurfaced, one after another—

about how impossible it had been to live with their mother, who believed the end of the world was near. How had they thought they could return to that prison to escape the problems in their current home?

Max set aside their phone on the nightstand. Rolling onto their side, they stared at Jo's sleeping body. For a long moment, they thought about touching her shoulder, waking her up, asking her if they were enough.

But the longer they stared, the more deeply they considered how exhausted she was and how much sleep she needed. Love sometimes meant forsaking one's insecurities to do what the beloved needed, and right now, that meant letting her be.

The achy hollowness they felt left them restless. They wondered about the voices Jo had heard, the reason why she didn't want to get married, and the cold rejection from their mother. They stared at the darkness in the room, absent of any moonlight through the plantation shutters, and worried if they would ever find rest.

After lying awake for minutes or hours, they sighed and rolled out of bed. In the bathroom, they found a bottle of melatonin in the medicine cabinet and took a large enough dose to get through the night.

"You can't just leave when the going gets tough," Candy said. "That's when you double down and stay."

Max held the umbrella over Candy's head as the two of them strode around the perimeter of The Spirit Store during a ten-minute break. The rain was more of an annoying drizzle, but neither Max nor Candy wanted to get wet. Max breathed in the cool, moist air, thinking of their text conversation with their mother last night, and wondered if Candy was right—by asking to move back home, they were shirking their responsibility.

"Then what do I do if I stay?"

"You make her life better." Candy stopped beside the back door to the store. She glanced at Max with a furrowed brow. "When you switched, Jo paid for counseling to get you out of your depression. It's your turn to ask what she needs and give it to her."

"But I don't have the same type of resources she has," Max said.

"You don't need to," Candy said. "When my wife was dying, I didn't have money to pay for experimental treatments that might or might not have worked. But I did have time, and I gave all of it to her."

Max opened the back door and allowed Candy to duck inside. For a passing moment, they stood underneath the threshold, closed the umbrella, and shook off the droplets. They didn't know what Jo needed or wanted, but they would do what Candy had suggested and ask.

That night, when Max stepped inside the warm house, they noticed Jo's purse on the coffee table and her heels beside the sofa. She was pacing back and forth, her arms behind her back, just like Joe used to do when trying to solve a problem.

"What's wrong?" Max asked.

She didn't say.

"Did something happen at work?"

Again, no answer.

Sighing, Max remembered their conversation with Candy. They stood beside her pacing body and asked, "What do you need from me?"

Jo stopped walking and raised her gaze. Her eyes were red and swollen, like she had been crying for hours. "It's too late for you to do anything."

The comment stung like an insult. "I don't understand." Max took a step forward and touched her shoulder. "Too late for what?"

"For everything." She shook off their hand and resumed pacing. After a while, she gulped, and a fresh batch of tears streamed down her cheeks.

A feeling of helplessness overcame Max. They handed her a tissue from the box on the coffee table even though they wanted to leave.

Jo batted away their hand and darted down the hallway to the guest bathroom. The toilet seat clanked against the tank.

Plunk-plunk-plunk.

Max winced, listening to the sounds of vomit hitting the water. They shuffled into the bathroom, only to witness Jo heaving once again.

"Is it the flu?" they asked.

She sank back onto her heels, resting her forehead on the edge of the toilet seat. Her arms gripped the sides of the tank. "No."

"Then what is it?"

With one hand, she waved toward the sink.

Max glanced in the general direction. They noticed something on the counter—a white stick with two blue lines. They gasped. "You're pregnant?"

Without a word, Jo heaved once again, but only bile projected from her mouth.

Max grabbed a face towel from the rack and ran the tap until warm water pulsed against the cloth. They wrung it out and placed it against Jo's forehead. "Do you need to go to the doctor?"

Jo shook her head and slowly stood, handing Max the washcloth.

Max tossed the damp face towel on the counter and wrapped an arm around Jo's waist and guided her out of the bathroom. They led her to the primary bedroom and eased her into bed. In the adjoining bathroom, they ran the tap again and moistened another washcloth. They wrung the excess water and laid the folded-up towel against Jo's forehead.

In the kitchen, they poured a glass of water and toasted a slice of bread and brought both on a tray to the bedroom. They placed the tray on the nightstand and offered Jo the glass of water.

"Thanks." Jo propped herself against two pillows and accepted the glass with both hands.

Max had so many questions, but they knew not to ask. Not right now. They sat next to Jo and waited as she drank the glass of water, sip by sip, as the waning light of day left the room.

CHAPTER 26

"I'm going to be a father."

Max sat at an outdoor café with their mother. The autumnal sun cast an ethereal glow over the table, where their cups of coffee cooled. They had taken Jo's advice to break the news in person and Candy's advice to meet at a neutral location. They stared at their mother's intent face, waiting for a response. Every muscle tensed in their body, fearful of her reaction.

Finally, after what felt like minutes, she took a sip of her coffee and spoke. "I thought I'd taught you to be careful." She cradled the cup in her hands, her lips steeled into a straight line. "How can you be so irresponsible as to bring a child into this mess of a world?"

"Is that how you and Dad felt about making me?" The words sounded sharp and brittle in their ears, and they seized a paper napkin from the table and shred it strip by strip in their lap.

Their mother's eyebrows shot upward as her eyes widened and her nostrils flared. "Who told you how we felt about having you?"

"No one." Max narrowed their gaze. "I guessed from how you always treat me."

"And how is that?"

"With disdain." They spat the final word out like choking up a piece of meat lodged in their throat. Shame and disappointment burned through their skin, more powerfully than the pale sunshine. Dipping their head toward their chest, they gathered the bits of the destroyed napkin into a crumpled ball and squeezed until their fingers hurt. "Will you ever love me or approve of anything I do?"

In the following moments, the sounds of brakes from wheezing cars and the sharp call of migrating birds surrounded the intimate scene of mother and adult child. Max set the balled-up mess of a napkin on the table. The strands of paper came apart and fluttered away in the slight breeze. They didn't move to pick up the litter, but they noticed their mother's frown deepen as her gaze tracked the errant strips across the pavement and into the street.

"I thought I would be happy, having a child," she finally said. She shook her head and sighed. "I wasn't cut out to parent, but your father was. He was happy we had you."

"I know," Max said.

"But I fell into a postpartum depression that just deepened over the years." She fiddled with the handle of her coffee mug. "When your father died, something finally broke inside of me." Her eyes filled with tears, and she fixed her gaze on Max. "I'm sorry."

The words, unexpected and heartfelt, shattered all expectations.

Max stretched an arm across the table and patted the back of their mother's hand. "I didn't want to be a father. The whole thing was an accident."

The embryo had been conceived before Patty's

celebration of life, before their birthday, before either Jo or Max had spoken of the possibility. Max didn't know the exact moment, but they suspected it had happened one careless night when neither one of them bothered to check the expiration date on a box of condoms. They were in a hurry, and Jo reached in her nightstand drawer.

"I used to use these before I met you," she had said, tossing a foil wrapper between them on the mattress.

When Jo had finally gone to Max's former OB-GYN, she was already too far along for an abortion. She said she would carry the child to term, but Max had noticed she lacked the enthusiasm she'd once had when the possibility of having a child was only a wish or a fantasy.

But Max had been surprised by the growing fondness for the life inside Jo. They had quit working at The Spirit Store a week before Halloween to tend to Jo's morning sickness that prevented her from arriving at the office early and the fatigue that kept her from staying too late. Jo rebelled against the restrictions imposed by her body, lashing out at Max, straining their already-fragile relationship.

"But I'm happy now," Max said, squeezing their mother's hand. "I'm looking forward to being the parent I always wanted for a child who deserves the best I have to give."

Nodding, their mother returned the pressure with her hand. "You'll be a good parent," she said. "You not only look like your father, but you share the same heart he had."

"Everything looks normal," Dr. Lux said. She removed the stethoscope and typed a few notes into Jo's medical file. "I suggest you take it easy and stop worrying."

Max slumped in the visitor's chair beside the examination table. They glanced from the doctor with her no-nonsense attitude to Jo, who shivered beneath the blue paper gown. They had come to hear the baby's heartbeat, to ask the doctor questions Jo might have missed, and to be the partner they would have wanted if the tables had been turned.

"What about the voices?" Jo asked, crossing her arms over her chest.

"Stress and worry can cause someone to hear voices." Dr. Lux scribbled something on a prescription pad, tore it off, and handed it to Jo. "I recommend counseling, a prenatal vitamin, and mandatory time off from work."

Jo gaped at the piece of paper. "I can't take time off. I'm developing something important with my new company."

"What's more important than your health and the well-being of the life growing inside you?"

Jo glanced at Max before dropping her gaze to the floor. "Okay," she muttered. "But once I stop hearing voices, may I return to work?"

"Let's schedule your next appointment in four weeks, and we'll see how you are at that time. If anything changes before then, come back immediately."

As soon as the doctor exited, Jo flung the paper across the room. It fluttered like a broken wing before skittering next to Max's feet. They bent, plucking the paper from the floor. Squinting, they read the words on the page.

Prenatal counseling—12 weeks
Prenatal vitamin—once daily
Leave from work—indefinitely

Max tucked the paper in their breast pocket and stood.

Shuffling over to Jo, they placed a hand on her shoulder. "It's temporary."

Jo shrugged off their hand and hopped down from the examination table. She ripped off the blue paper gown and shoved her legs into her underwear before shimmying into her work dress. The material stretched tight across her midsection, and Max knew she would soon have to abandon her business suits for maternity wear.

"I have investors depending on my input on the project," Jo said while Max steered her out of the examination room and down the hallway to the parking lot. "I can't let Eli do it alone."

"He's not alone," Max said, pushing the button to activate the automatic doors.

A gust of cool air blew into the walkway, and they shivered. The temperature had dropped suddenly over the past few days—from record-high nineties to the low fifties. A pall of rain clouds hung low in the gray sky.

Max glanced over at Jo, gauging her mood. Squeezing her elbow, they guided her toward the car. "You have a whole team supporting him." They forced a smile, hoping to inject a bit of brightness into the situation. "Candy starts tomorrow. She's a quick study. I'm sure she'll be a great addition to the team."

"Don't remind me of that woman." Jo shook her arm out of Max's grasp. "I only hired her because she's your friend and Eli's lover."

"You won't regret it," Max promised. With a click of the fob, they unlocked the car doors and held one open for Jo.

She groaned, sliding into the passenger seat. "What's happened to me? I've gone against everything I used to practice."

Nodding, Max sank into the driver's seat and started the engine. They remembered Joe's policy of no nepotism. Part of them was glad that practical side had disappeared in the haze of hormones.

Jo rubbed her temples with her fingertips. "I can't believe the doctor dismissed the voices."

"You didn't tell her about the failed brain-to-brain experiment puncturing the divide between this world and the next," Max said.

They steered out of the parking lot and merged into the evening traffic. They stayed in the slow lane since their reflexes were slower. Under the circumstances, they felt they were the better driver.

Jo banged her fist against the dashboard. "I know what I heard and why I heard it."

Max had neither heard the voices nor intercepted Jo's thoughts, so they could not confirm or deny Jo's declaration. Taking a side street, they drove past houses—a patchwork quilt of leftover Halloween decorations amid gold and brown leaves.

"I'm wondering if we can invite my mother to Thanksgiving next week. I'll make a turkey and all the fixings. She can bring dessert. She used to make a great peach cobbler."

"Peach cobbler for Thanksgiving?"

"Don't knock it till you try it. It's better than pumpkin pie." Max pulled into their driveway and pressed the button to activate the garage door. "She stopped making it after my father died, but I'm sure she'll make it again if I ask." The last part was a lie. Max didn't know if their mother would make anything, but they were banking on Jo not being able to hear their thoughts.

"Fine, but I'll bake a pumpkin pie just in case."

Max's pulse spiked a notch, and they parked the car in the garage. "So, that's a yes?"

Jo released the seat belt and cracked open the door. The stuffy air floated into the cab, and the weak overhead light from the rafters cast shadows on her face. "Why not? The more, the merrier." She slid out of the car and strode up the steps into the house.

As the engine *tick-tick-ticked* as it cooled, Max leaned back against the driver's seat. They didn't care if Jo was a wet blanket. A warmth flooded their chest. This dinner would mark the first holiday celebration since their father had died, and nothing and no one would ruin it.

CHAPTER 27

Two days before Thanksgiving, Max woke up, hearing the voice of their unborn child.

Daddy, it's Ru.

Max blinked three times and focused their watery gaze in the direction of the voice, which seemed to come from the corner of the room nearest to Jo. In the faint gray light leaking beneath the bedroom window, they could make out only shadows and empty space.

Ru? They thought the child's name, too afraid to speak aloud and wake Jo.

It's short for Rupert. I'm named after your father.

Max shifted against the pillows. They had not heard from their father in months. When the voices stopped, they assumed they would never return. Now that communication had reopened between this world and the next, Max wondered, *How is he?*

Divine.

The single-worded response triggered an ironic reaction in Max. Instead of inspiring hope and faith and love, a shiver of fear ran through their body. Who felt divine? No one Max knew. They had expected a standard response, like *good* or *fine.*

Maybe they were still dreaming. They rolled onto

their side and stared at Jo's back. Her body rose and fell in time with her even breathing. From what Max could tell, she was sleeping. They didn't know what time it was, but from behind them, the ethereal glow from the perimeter of the window suggested the moments before sunrise.

Just before hearing the voice, they had been dreaming about cradling a small bundle in their arms while they swayed from side to side in a sterile-smelling hospital room. Bells rang from the church down the street, and Jo rested in a hospital bed, her hair plastered against her flushed face, her arms limp and her body spent. An expansive feeling flooded their chest as they rocked the newborn in their arms. Love. Not the love they felt for Jo—which undulated, like waves on a sea of romantic expectations—but a steady, free-flowing love that pulsed like a heartbeat. They might not have wanted this child, but they loved the baby just the same, if not more than they had loved anyone in their life.

They blinked several times to clear their watery vision. Slowly, the features of the familiar room took shape—the short hall to the bathroom, the doors of the closet, the bureau against the wall with the TV mounted above it. Clearly, they were no longer dreaming. The voice they'd heard was real, as real as their father's voice and Patty's voice had been all those months ago.

Where are you? they asked their child.

Here in the corner above Mommy.

Max glanced at the corner nearest Jo. Nothing hovered where the walls intersected the ceiling. Nothing but empty space.

I don't see you.

I'm here.

Max felt that same feeling of reassurance they felt

once they knew the voices of Patty and their father were real. But they wanted to know more. Just to be sure. Because this experience was so foreign.

Where do you come from?

The beforelife.

Beforelife?

A section of heaven where baby beings wait to be born.

The concept of hundreds of thousands of baby beings jostling in a waiting room seemed as unlikely and as ridiculous as the concept of an afterlife, where billions of beings crowded into the ether beyond the visible universe. But where else was this voice coming from?

Max rolled onto their back and folded their hands over their chest. They listened to their jagged breathing, which seemed to rise and fall in an erratic manner compared to Jo's slow, even breath. Every now and then, they glanced at the corner of the room, where the baby being supposedly hovered, invisible but audible.

Your mother seems to think she hears voices. They tried to stop their thoughts, but they dashed ahead without compulsion. *Is it true?* They held their breath, waiting, hoping, praying it was not true.

I don't know.

A rush of breath exhaled from their lips, and their heartbeat ratcheted in their chest. They balled their hands against the covers. *What do you mean, you don't know? You're in heaven. Don't you know everything?*

I only know what God wants me to know.

Sighing, Max exhaled sharply. They released their hands and flexed their feet and wiggled their toes. They didn't like the answer, even if it was truthful. Maybe they needed to approach the topic from a different angle and find someone from the afterlife instead of the beforelife who might know this information.

Have you seen my father, your grandfather?

Of course. He's the one who suggested I come.

Can you ask him what Jo heard?

No, I can't. I can't talk to him anymore. I'm here. Waiting. I can only talk to you. I've tried talking to Mom, but she can't hear me.

Max frowned at Jo's back, wondering if this news was true. Had she blocked out all information between this world and the next?

Help me, Max thought. *I'm trying to understand the logic of heaven.*

At first, Max feared the baby being might protest and give another excuse about not knowing, but the answer came quickly. They had to ask their soon-to-be child to repeat it so they could be sure of what was said.

I'm here to heal your mother's broken heart.

A tenderness spread throughout Max's body. They rolled onto their side and cupped a hand over Jo's abdomen. She wasn't showing much, and it was too early to feel the fetus moving beneath the skin, but Max hoped the warmth of their hand could communicate their love and longing for everything this baby-to-be-born promised.

"Thanks for inviting me."

Max heard their mother's voice when Jo answered the front door. They had just removed the turkey and placed it on the quartz counter to settle before carving.

Jo ushered Max's mother into the room, taking the peach cobbler from her outstretched arms.

As soon as Max saw their mother, they wiped their

hands on a dish towel before flinging their arms around their mother's back and pressing her close to their chest. "Mom, it's good to see you again. Thanks for coming." They sniffed her talcum-powder-scented skin, mingled with the sweetness of canned peaches, and felt transported home.

She wriggled free and held them by the shoulders, surveying every detail of their face. "I love looking at you. You remind me of your father."

The love in her voice calmed any nervousness Max might have felt.

They took her coat and led her to the dining room table. "Have a seat."

While carving the turkey, Max mused on the months between when they had moved out of their mother's house as a young woman to when they had moved into the house they shared with Jo as an old man. It felt weird and awkward at times, like trying to learn the steps to a new dance, but at other times, it felt as natural as breathing.

"Did Max tell you our good news?" Jo asked, serving their mother a cup of cider.

"About the baby?" She glanced over at Max and smiled. "Yes, they did. I'm going to be a grandma."

"In May," Jo said, taking the seat beside her.

"Will you get married?" Max's mother glanced from Jo to Max. "A baby needs a family."

Jo bit her lower lip and twisted her hands in her lap. She was wearing a loose dress to hide the slight swell in her abdomen. "Max has asked, but I keep saying no."

"Why?"

Shrugging, Jo released her hands.

Max placed the carved turkey on the table, along with

the potatoes, gravy, stuffing, Brussels sprouts, butternut squash, cranberry sauce, and rolls.

They nudged their mother's arm and winked. "She doesn't want to be tied down."

"Hogwash." Their mother shook her head. "A child will tie you down. A marriage is a support system. Without it, the whole enterprise will collapse."

"What about single parents?" Jo asked. "They seem to do just fine on their own."

"Sure, let the media tell you that's the case. Then let's talk about the statistics."

"No, let's not." Max placed a hand on their mother's shoulder and squeezed. "No talk." They didn't want to hear about everything they had avoided since moving out —the conspiracy theories, the scientific data, the expert opinions, and public polls. They wanted the intimacy of peace and ignorance in the blissfulness of a good meal in the warmth and comfort of their home with the two people—three, counting Ru—they loved more than anyone in the world.

Nodding, their mother bowed her head to silently pray.

Jo shrugged an apology.

Max sank into the chair next to their mother and started serving, handing one dish after another until everyone had their plates full.

Halfway through dinner, Jo glanced at Max's mother and asked, "If we have a girl, may we name her after you?"

She gulped and stared wide-eyed at one, then the other. "You want to name her Pearl?"

"If you don't mind," Jo said.

"No, of course not. That would be nice," Pearl said. "And if it's a boy?"

"Rupert, of course," Max said, smiling. They didn't want to spoil the surprise by letting everyone know they had already spoken to the child and knew they were having a boy. Jo had decided to be old-fashioned and wait until the baby was born to learn the gender. "We'll call him Ru for short."

"Ru," their mother mused aloud. "That's what I called your father."

In the silence that followed, Max marveled at the curious comfort at the table. Jo and Pearl were strangers, but Max was the common denominator between them. They had expected to feel tense and uncertain, navigating the distance between what was said and what was felt yet unspoken, but the sounds of silverware clicking against the plates, punctuated by soft chewing, blanketed the gathering with a subtle yet profound sense of ease. Max wondered why they had fought against uniting these two sides of their life—the before with their mother and the after with Jo and the baby—until now. Lifting their glass of water to their lips, they thought about the bounty of their blessings and felt their heart fill with gratitude and peace.

CHAPTER 28

"Oh, I felt something." Jo dropped the Christmas ornament into the box and folded her hands over her abdomen.

Max rushed over to her side, almost tripping on a string of lights they had strung halfway up the artificial Christmas tree. Dr. Lux had suggested getting rid of the spruce they had bought once Jo couldn't stop sneezing.

"Is it the baby?"

Smiling, she grabbed their hand and placed it over the slight swell below her waist. "Can you feel it?"

Frowning, Max rubbed their palm back and forth across the space. "No."

"It feels like butterfly wings."

Butterfly wings? The thought amazed them.

"The fetus is probably still too small for you to feel."

Max tried to remember what size the fetus was at sixteen weeks. They had read something in the pregnancy book their mother had bought them, but their short-term memory wasn't as good as it used to be.

"She's the size of an avocado," Jo said.

"She?" Max tugged away their hand. "The baby talked to me and told me it was a boy."

"I told you I didn't want to know the baby's gender."

The heat of Jo's anger burned brightly, and Max took a step back. "Sorry."

Jo grumbled, flopping onto the sofa. She scrubbed her face with both hands. "I hate how you keep forgetting things I tell you."

"Me too." Max nudged aside a box of decorations with their foot.

"I know it's not your fault." She dropped her hands into her lap. "You're old—that's all."

But Max sometimes wondered and worried they were developing dementia.

"So, tell me, when did you speak to our child?"

The question swiveled Max's attention back to the conversation. "Before Thanksgiving."

"Why didn't you tell me?" Jo frowned, and the V between her eyebrows deepened.

Max shuffled around the boxes of ornaments and sat next to her. "I didn't want to bother you or scare you since you'd said you'd been hearing voices." They paused. "You know, you never told me who was talking to you or what they said."

She glanced away, staring at the hardwood floor.

The wall that had erected in Jo's mind suddenly gave way, and Max could hear her thoughts.

Your father said you would die soon.

Max stiffened with the realization that Jo had lied by omission. She was being protective, shielding them from the truth, but the effort only reminded them of their meddlesome mother, pushing an agenda they didn't want. For a long moment, they sat, not thinking, only feeling a sense of betrayal spread over their aching limbs like a weighted blanket—pinning them beneath things they didn't want to acknowledge, but couldn't ignore.

Finally, they slapped their palms against their thighs and stood, grunting. The old-man sound reminded them of their grandfather, who hadn't talked much but who grumbled like a slow-moving river every time they bent or stood.

"I miss the smell of a real tree," Jo said, breaking the silence.

Nodding, Max removed a stick of incense from another box beside the tree and lit it. Soon, the smell of pine filled the room.

"You think of everything, don't you?" Jo said.

Max fiddled with the string of lights, weaving them through the branches until they couldn't reach any higher. The bottom half of the tree winked, and the top half of the tree stood, darkened.

"Why did you lie to me?"

"About what?" The V between her eyebrows deepened like a permanent groove.

"The voice you heard was my father, telling you I would die soon." Max dropped the remaining strand of white lights and hobbled into the utility closet for the stepladder. They climbed until they were tall enough to circle the rest of the tree with blinking lights.

Frowning, Jo crossed her arms over her chest. "How dare you barge into my thoughts?"

"Me?" Max clambered down the stepladder. "That's rich. Blaming me for the flawed technology you developed."

"Not every experiment succeeds," she said, standing.

Max scoffed. "You sound like Dr. Dio." They folded the stepladder and placed it back in the closet. "I'm not a child. You don't need to shield me from the truth." They straightened their back, but their voice broke into a wobbly sob.

"Oh, Max." Jo strode across the room. She wrapped her arms around their back and tugged them against her breasts. "I'm sorry."

"Why did you do it?" Their voice was muffled.

She sighed. "I didn't want to parent without you."

"Is that why you turned down my marriage proposal?"

She squeezed tighter, nodding her chin against their head.

"Well, I'm not going anywhere," Max said, resting their cheek between her breasts. They felt Jo's heartbeat thud against their jaw, and they held her tighter. "Don't you understand? There is no division between life and death. Everything exists on a continuation. Whether you can hear me or not."

She rubbed her hand against their back. "I wish I could believe you."

Max didn't know how to explain to Jo that they didn't just believe. They knew. Life stretched into infinity. A beforelife, where baby beings waited to be born. The life they were living now. And the afterlife, where they would go to meet their maker.

They stepped back and kissed Jo's temple, trying to reassure her. "It doesn't matter when I die. Tomorrow or ten years from now. I promise I'll be here to raise our child, one way or another, from this world or the next."

A week before Christmas, while browsing through baby clothes, Max sneezed. It was just a tickle in the back of their throat. They didn't think anything of it.

But the day before Christmas, the tickle had grown

from an itch into a raging cough. They heard the wheezing in their chest—a hollow whistle, ending in a rattle.

Afraid to get Jo sick, they slept in the guest bedroom until they could visit the doctor.

"It's pneumonia," Dr. Chavez said, removing the stethoscope from her ears. "I'll prescribe an antibiotic for ten days. If you don't feel better in a couple of days, come and see me again."

Max picked up the prescription at the pharmacy and drove home, all along thinking, *This is it. This is the beginning of the end Jo feared.*

But on Christmas morning, they felt better. The cough had eased. They could breathe without the air rattling inside their lungs.

At dinner, sitting across from Jo and their mother, they enjoyed the meal all of them had cooked. Ham and potatoes and green bean casserole with Pearl's famous peach cobbler, topped with whipped cream, for dessert.

"Dr. Lux released me to return to work after the holidays," Jo announced.

She was the picture of health, glowing from the inside out.

Pearl passed the rolls around the table, followed by a tray of butter. "I came from an era where women didn't work while they were pregnant. I don't know how you do it. I just didn't have the energy."

"I feel so much energy that I get in Max's way around the home." She glanced at Max. "Aren't I, hon?"

The heat of embarrassment traveled over Max's face. "Yes, you are." They didn't want their mother to know the details of Jo's insatiable appetite for life and how it affected the intimacy of their relationship, so they tried to keep it simple. "Everywhere I go, there you are."

Pearl nodded. "And what will you be doing, Max?"

"Getting ready for the baby. I'm turning the guest bedroom into the nursery."

"That gives me an idea," Pearl said. "How about I turn your old bedroom into a nursery?" She smiled, and her face flushed. "You two might want to get away every once in a while, and I can keep the baby overnight at my house."

"Sounds good," Jo said. "Doesn't it, hon?"

The thought of their mother taking care of their child brought back the conversation they'd had with Ru weeks ago. About how he was here to heal their mother's heart. Max smiled, witnessing the enthusiasm in their mother's voice, the joy in her facial expression, and the hope in her offer.

"That would be perfect," Max said. And they meant it.

CHAPTER 29

O n the first day back to work, Jo slipped into a fashionable maternity dress and posed before the full-length mirror she had installed on the back of the bedroom door. "What do you think?"

Max glanced at the berry-colored sweater dress and shrugged. "Everything looks good on you. You have the curves I never had."

"Jealous, are we?" Jo winked, then kissed their cheek. "What will you do with your time now that I'll be gone for nine hours a day?"

"I'll have to check my honey-do list," Max half teased.

A light perspiration broke out across their skin. They had started writing a to-do list every night and posting it on the refrigerator door since they could no longer rely on their short-term memory.

"Well, as long as dinner is hot and ready on the table when I get home, I don't care how you spend your time," Jo said.

Max served Jo breakfast (hot decaffeinated coffee, protein pancakes with extra maple syrup) and packed up her lunch (a sensible chef salad with buttermilk ranch dressing in its own container) and kissed her goodbye. Once the garage door rattled closed, they consulted the to-do list posted on the refrigerator door.

1. Buy life insurance.
2. Decorate nursery.
3. Water plants.
4. Do laundry.
5. Go grocery shopping.
6. Cook dinner.

The list was simple, something anyone younger could memorize. They picked up the phone and called their insurance carrier to discuss life insurance policies.

"I'm sorry," the insurance agent said. "But you're ineligible. We don't insure against Acts of God."

"I thought it was a preexisting medical condition," Max said, tapping the end of the pen against the notepad.

"No, for insurance purposes, the switch is considered an Act of God."

After they ended the call, they sat on the sofa, staring at the floor. Almost a year since the first person had switched, and no one knew what had caused it. A feeling of unbearable sadness washed over them. Would anyone ever know?

Glancing around the great room at the dining table, where they shared family meals, to the kitchen, where they cooked every day, to the window overlooking the backyard, where they gardened during better weather, they breathed in deeply and listened to the clearness in their chest. They had no reason to worry, no reason to feel depressed, and yet a persistent undercurrent of sorrow traveled throughout their body. They set aside the list and stood, stretching the aches from their arms and legs, before grabbing the piece of paper and getting on with the rest of the tasks for the day.

By the time daffodils sprouted in the backyard, Max had felt their child rolling around like a marble beneath Jo's tight skin. They decorated the nursery in gender-neutral colors—muted yellows and buttery whites.

When they visited their mother for a weekly lunch at her house, they marveled at the transformation of their former bedroom. The walls had been painted a soft blush. A crib replaced the twin bed. A changing table was situated beside the window overlooking the backyard, where Max had once sat at a desk, typing their essays for school. Only the dresser remained. It was full of baby clothes, receiving blankets, and cloth diapers.

"You know they have disposable diapers," Max said.

"Oh, I won't use those," she said. "I'll wash these, like I did for you."

Max shook their head, but didn't comment on the extra work, not wanting to spark a discussion about the hazards of disposable diapers on the environment. Instead, they turned their attention to the photographs of family members as babies their mother had hung on the walls. They didn't recognize anyone except themselves.

"That's your aunt and your cousin and your father," their mother said, pointing to one photograph after another. "And this one is me." A baby girl, sitting on a blanket and holding a rattle, beamed with a toothless grin back at Max.

"You were cute," Max said, smiling. "I hope our child is as cute."

Their mother placed a hand on Max's arm. "I'm sure he or she will be the cutest baby you've ever seen."

Gazing into their mother's hopeful eyes, Max widened their smile. They patted the back of their mother's hand. "It's good to see you happy again."

Nodding, their mother grinned. "It's good to have something to look forward to."

"Look." Candy stretched her arm across the table at the café where she met Max for their weekly cup of coffee on Sunday mornings.

Max set down their cup of coffee and squinted. They needed reading glasses now, but they hadn't bothered to get a prescription or buy one of those over-the-counter reading glasses found at any drugstore. "What am I looking for?"

"Are you blind?" Candy wiggled her fingers. "Can't you see the bling?"

Ugh. Max hated all the slang Candy picked up from her granddaughter. They grasped the tips of her fingers and turned her hand from side to side. Rainbow colors dazzled across their field of vision once the object caught a beam from the recessed lighting.

"A ring?"

"Not just any ring. An engagement ring from Eli." Candy withdrew her hand and bounced up and down in her seat. "We're getting married next summer."

A tightness formed in their chest, and they swallowed. "Congratulations."

Candy's eyes glittered with happiness. She cupped her hands around her mug and smiled. "We were going to get married earlier, but we didn't want to upstage the birth of your baby."

The baby was due three weeks after Jo's birthday. Max

felt time slowing, with each day longer than the last. Jo was still working. She had insisted she would start her maternity leave the moment her water broke, which left Max with endless time after the daily chores were done. Except for the lunches with their mother and their coffees with Candy, most of their days unfolded in solid repetition, indistinguishable from one another.

"I thought you would be happier," Candy said.

Max shrugged. "Nothing excites me like it used to," they said. "I don't know why."

"I used to get that way sometimes," Candy said. "I think it's the fatigue that comes with being older. Have you tried cutting down on your activities?"

"No." Max fiddled with a napkin, twisting the edges. "I have too much to do with the baby coming."

"Well, maybe you should start taking afternoon naps." Candy finished her coffee and pushed her mug aside. "I used to take a twenty-minute nap every day. It saved me." She tilted her head to the side, and her hair fell against her shoulder. She had let it grow over the winter, and the shaggy mane suited her. "It's good training for when the baby comes. My wife and I only slept when the baby napped."

That sadness that had only come in waves seemed to wash up against everything now. Its persistent presence dampened any enthusiasm Max might have felt.

They shrugged again. "I'm sure my mom will be coming over to help."

"Eli and I can come over, too, but only on the weekends. We've a tight deadline at work. Jo wants to roll out the product as soon as we get government approval." Candy's phone vibrated on the table. She flipped it over and swiped the screen. "I need to go soon. Eli and I are going to his mother's house this afternoon to announce our engagement." She met Max's gaze. "Will you be my man of honor?"

"What about Sarah?" Max asked, thinking a maid of honor would be better.

"I'm not close to Sarah like I am with you. She's my granddaughter, not my best friend."

Max stared at the pleading look Candy gave. They didn't like Eli, even though they had learned to tolerate him, but they did love Candy like the sibling they'd never had but always wanted. "Sure. Do you want me in a dress or a tux?"

Candy laughed. "Wear whatever you want."

"A tux. I have your old one, and I know it fits."

CHAPTER 30

Max was writing a shopping list for tonight's dinner—chicken breast, broccoli, bell pepper, and white rice—when they heard their father's voice.

It's time.

I don't want to go.

Max dropped the pen, which fell against the hardwood floor and rolled under the dishwasher. They bent at the knees, then the waist before stretching their arm and wiggling their fingers, but the pen remained out of reach. They straightened, and their joints ached. Their gaze skittered to the calendar on the refrigerator door.

How about after the baby is born?

I'm not in charge of that decision.

Who is?

God, of course.

Well, can you ask him to give me more time? Dr. Lux said first babies are often late, and I want to be at the birth.

I've already asked time and again. You need to leave now.

No—

A sudden pain seized Max beneath their sternum.

A warning flashed across their mind like a ticker tape at the bottom of a TV screen. *Call 911.* Max fumbled with the cell phone, but it tumbled out of their hand and skittered across the hardwood floor and settled next to the pen. Just out of reach.

In the stillness of the kitchen, Max clutched a fist against their chest and worried about everything they would miss. The first light of day, the sourness of morning breath, the roughness of a goodbye kiss. The fluorescent glare in the grocery store. The sticky wheels of a shopping cart dragged against the slick linoleum floor. The smell of freshly minced garlic and diced onions. The sharp taste of the costly porcini-champignon sea salt they had bought at the tiny boutique store in Montgomery Village, which brought out the layers of flavor in asparagus sautéed in olive oil. The lingering glow of pastel colors swiped across the evening sky. The comfort of the familiar *flip-flap-flop* shuffle of their feet against the hardwood floor. The coolness of the soft sheets and the warmth of Jo's skin. The *thump-thump-thump* of the baby's knees and elbows poking across the surface of Jo's swollen belly. The creaking dip of the mattress whenever Jo got up to pee in the middle of the night. The hollow emptiness of the sleepless moments before dawn.

How could Max leave all of that?

But Max had no choice. A headache exploded with dizzying terror, and their legs collapsed. Max tried to grasp the ledge of the kitchen counter but missed. At the precise moment their body fell on the hardwood floor, their spirit dislodged from the elderly casing and soared

> up,
>
> up,
>
> up,
>
> higher

and
higher,
until they reached a cloudy embankment, where they met a shimmering display of dazzling light.

"Dad?" They shimmied closer.

"Here," Dad said. "You're finally here."

Dad embraced Max.

The magnitude of their combined energies brightened and glowed.

"Welcome, my child of light."

No longer hostage to a human body, Max was neither man nor woman.

Max was light, and light was Max.

www.ingramcontent.com/pod-product-compliance
Lightning Source LLC
Chambersburg PA
CBHW022040240626
47154CB00007B/2503